GIRL
WITH A
CAMERA

GIRL
WITH A
CAMERA

Margaret Bourke-White perches with her camera on a Chrysler Building gargoyle sixty-one floors above the streets of New York City.

GIRL WITH A CAMERA

Margaret Bourke-White,
Photographer

A NOVEL

CAROLYN MEYER

CALKINS CREEK
AN IMPRINT OF HIGHLIGHTS
Honesdale, Pennsylvania

Calkins Creek
An Imprint of Highlights
815 Church Street
Honesdale, Pennsylvania 18431

Printed in the United States of America
ISBN: 978-1-62979-584-3 (HC)
ISBN: 978-1-62979-800-4 (e-book)
Library of Congress Control Number: 2016951193

First edition
The text of this book is set in Neutraface.
Design by Anahid Hamparian
Production by Sue Cole
10 9 8 7 6 5 4 3 2 1

For Vered and Giovanny

Prologue

Sometime after midnight, a thump—loud and jarring. A torpedo slams into the side of our ship, flinging me out of my bunk. The ship is transporting thousands of troops and hundreds of nurses. It is December 1942, and our country is at war. I am Margaret Bourke-White, the only woman photographer covering this war.

The U.S. Army Air Forces has handed me a plum assignment: photographing an Allied attack on German troops in North Africa. I wanted to fly in one of our B-17 bombers, but the top brass ordered me to travel instead on the flagship of a huge convoy, headed from England through the Strait of Gibraltar toward the coast of North Africa. It would be safer than flying, the officers argued.

As it turns out, they were dead wrong. Beneath the surface of the Mediterranean, German submarines glide, silent and lethal, stalking their prey. We are asleep when one of their torpedoes finds its mark.

The ship tilts sharply, and the lights flicker and die. I pull on my olive drab work slacks and my officer's coat, thinking it will be warmer than the waterproof trench coat. Fumbling in the dark, I grab my musette bag with one camera and, leaving everything else behind, race to the bridge to try to photograph what is happening, but there is not enough light and not enough time. The order blares: "Abandon ship! Abandon ship!" I head for Lifeboat No. 12 and board with the others assigned to it, about fifty people, mostly nurses. We've drilled for it over and over, but this is not a drill. My mouth is dry with fear. Our boat is overloaded, but the officer in charge says we're going to chance it. As we are lowered, I can't help thinking what a dramatic photograph that view of our sinking ship would make, if only the light were better.

We sit up to our waists in water from the torpedo splash-back and use our helmets to bail. The rudder is broken. All around us in the water, people are thrashing and grabbing for something to hang on to, struggling to survive. We rescue some, lose others. A voice cries in the darkness, "Help me! I'm all alone!" We try to row toward that desperate voice, but without a rudder we can do nothing. The cries grow fainter. Then, silence.

I take my turn rowing, my arms aching and my hands blistered. Someone in a nearby lifeboat begins to sing "You Are My Sunshine." We all join in. Even off-key, it makes the rowing easier. We watch silently as flames swallow our wounded ship.

The rest of the convoy has scattered to keep from giving the German U-boats another target. In the bright moonlight I see that a single destroyer stays behind, and we hope they will come to pick us up. But no—they drop depth charges to try to get rid of any remaining German submarines. Someone is shouting into a megaphone, but we can't make out the words. Maybe he's wishing us luck. The destroyer sails on. No one in our boat says a word. Now we are entirely alone.

The moon sinks into the dark sea. I think longingly of chocolate bars, the emergency rations I'd tossed out of my camera bag to make room for extra lenses. The hours pass. I'm wet to the skin, and cold. Hungry, too. I could do with a bite of chocolate.

Dawn comes slowly, the pale colors blooming in the eastern sky. I wonder again if I will survive, if any of us will. Irrationally, I mourn the loss of my elegant cosmetics case, covered with beautiful ostrich skin and filled with ivory jars from Hong Kong. I can't imagine why it matters.

It's December 22—the winter solstice, someone reminds us, and that's why the sun is so late making its appearance. We cheer when it finally rises majestically from a flat gray sea.

I get out my camera and begin taking pictures. We look miserable and bedraggled, but we're alive.

One of the nurses jokes that she's ready to place her order for breakfast: two eggs, sunny-side up, no broken yolks, please.

"And hot coffee!" adds another. "Buttered toast!"

Wet, cold, exhausted, crowded in with dozens of others, more than the boat is meant to hold—all wondering what will happen to us, if we will live or die—I think of my home, my parents, those early years when I had no idea where life would take me, only that I wanted it to be bold and exciting, anything but what it was then. . . .

1

I BLAME EVERYTHING ON MY MOTHER. SHE STROVE for perfection, and nothing else satisfied her. There were rules, and we—my sister, my brother, and I—were expected to abide by them.

Mother decreed that we would not read the funny papers. She found nothing funny about them. "The comics will harm your mind and ruin your taste for good art," she said. One look at "Krazy Kat" or "Maggie and Jiggs" would surely begin the deterioration of our brains.

We were not allowed to visit friends who *did* read the funny papers. I imagined Sara Jane Cassidy and her brother, Tommy, who lived on the next block, sprawled on the floor with the Sunday papers, laughing at the antics of the Katzenjammer Kids.

Sara Jane was sympathetic. She sometimes smuggled the funny papers to school in her lunch box and let me have a guilty look at them while I ate my liverwurst sandwich.

Mother also dismissed movies as a waste of time. "Movies entertain much too easily," she said. "Far better to read a good book that stimulates the mind."

No card-playing. (Chess was different. Father taught all of us to play—even Roger, who was much younger.) *No gum-chewing.*

My sister, Ruth, two years older than I, complained about our mother's rules even more than I did. The one that bothered Ruth most: *No silk stockings.* Mother insisted on cotton stockings. Much more practical.

"They're so ugly!" Ruth wailed.

"The hard way is always the better way," Mother lectured, unmoved.

◆◆

Our family lived in Bound Brook, New Jersey. I was in eighth grade, and Ruth rode the trolley to Plainfield, where she attended high school. Roger was only six and had just been enrolled in first grade. The minute we came home, Mother wanted a report of everything that happened that day. If I told her about a quiz in geography, mentioning that we had to answer just ten questions out of a dozen, she pounced: "I hope you chose the ten hardest," she said, frowning until I said yes, I had picked the hard ones, and answered the easy ones too.

Then she smiled and said, "Good girl!" She hardly ever said that to Ruth, and almost never told little Roger how good he was. Roger hated school.

I was sick and tired of being a good girl. What thirteen-year-old girl wouldn't be?

When Ruth and I were both in grammar school, we had walked together to the four-room schoolhouse, balancing along the tops of fences. After Ruth moved on to high school, I missed having her walk home with me, and I did my high-wire act without her.

Two grades were assigned to each room with one teacher, so that in fifth grade I shared a classroom with the sixth grade.

By the time I was actually a sixth grader, I had absorbed most of their lessons, and every afternoon the teacher sent me to the cloakroom with a group of slow readers to tutor them. This made me popular with no one.

Seventh grade improved nothing.

My best friend, Tubby Luf, was tall and blond and thin as a straw. Tubby's name was Margaret, like mine, but when her younger sister was just learning to talk, it somehow came out as "Tubby," and it stuck.

"I like it," she said. "It's ironic."

Tubby was the kind of brainy girl who used words like *ironic*.

Mother would not allow nicknames. Her name was Minnie—her given name, she claimed, not a nickname. My father was Joseph, but she made an exception for him: she called him Joey. If she could call my father Joey, why could I not be Peggy, the name I favored?

"Because I named you Margaret." End of argument.

At school I was Peggy, but in the presence of my mother I must always be Margaret.

Mother insisted that we speak correctly—proper grammar, no slang or contractions—no *I'm* or *she's* or *isn't* or *wouldn't*. "It shows sloppiness of mind," Mother declared, "as well as lack of effort." Ruth whispered to me that Mother often slipped up and used contractions herself.

The other students looked at me as though I were an oddity. The cotton stockings, the bans on funny papers and chewing gum, on slang and contractions and nicknames—Ruth and I were misfits. How could we *not* be?

Mother herself spoke very well. Father also spoke well, when he spoke at all—he was a very quiet man. Sometimes I thought he talked so little because he was afraid he'd make a mistake, and Mother would correct him.

Ruth and I wondered what our parents were like when they

were young. We had a photograph of Minnie Bourke in a white shirtwaist with leg-of-mutton sleeves, and Mother had confessed that a shirtwaist was considered "not quite nice" at the time. In the picture she is standing by her bicycle. She was about to ride the bicycle to meet Joseph White. The Whites lived in the Bronx, and the Bourkes in lower Manhattan. They rode out into the country and read philosophy to each other. One day Minnie's bicycle chain broke, and there was no way to fix it.

"We left our bikes and hiked up the nearest mountain," Mother told us, "and that's when your father proposed."

Ruth and I thought their courtship was terribly romantic.

"Do you think he kissed her?" Ruth asked me.

"Well, of course he kissed her!" I said. "She said yes, and then they kissed."

Ruth was doubtful. "They were very proper. And Mother has told me over and over that I mustn't let a boy kiss me until we're married."

◆ ◆

Father, an engineer for a company that manufactured printing presses, invented ways to improve their efficiency. One invention changed the way funny papers were printed in color, a mechanism to align the edges of the various colored parts. This may not sound like much, but it saved the company a lot of money.

He'd designed the unusual house we lived in and built the huge stone fireplace with a mantel he'd sawed out of a tree. He planted gardens that included rare specimens, each labeled with its scientific name. He took me on nature walks in the woods nearby, pointing out things he wanted me to observe. I was comfortable with his silence.

Father knew all about snakes and lizards. When I was nine or ten, a snake slithered across our path, sensed us, and stopped. It flattened its neck and raised its head up like a cobra, hissing and striking. I clutched Father's hand.

"Harmless," he said. "Just a hognose. Some people call it a puff adder, but a hognose snake isn't a puff adder at all. Only the real ones, the African kind, are deadly. Watch him roll over and play dead."

The snake did just that. His mouth was open, his tongue hanging out. He certainly *looked* dead. "Turn him right side up," Father said. I wasn't too sure about this, but when I did, the snake rolled over "dead" again.

"Can we take him home?" I asked, and Father agreed and showed me how to pick him up. I wasn't afraid.

The hognose/puff adder was soon completely tame and liked to curl up on Mother's lap when she sat in her rocking chair to sew or read the newspaper, and Mother didn't mind. I named him Puffy.

"You could have come up with something more original," Ruth said. "*Puffy* seems rather childish."

I glared at her. She sounded like Mother—*No nicknames*. I looked up the snake's scientific name in one of Father's books: *Heterodon platirhinos*. He would remain Puffy.

On the day I took him to school, Puffy, frightened out of his wits, performed exactly as I knew he would, rearing up, neck puffed out, and hissing menacingly. The other children screamed and pulled away, even though I promised he wouldn't bite. They laughed nervously when he played dead, but still they refused to touch him.

"Do not be afraid, it is just a hognose," I reassured them.

My schoolmates reported "Margaret's poisonous snake" to the principal, who ordered me to take Puffy home and not to bring him or any other snake to school.

"There are only two venomous kinds of snakes in New Jersey—rattler and copperhead," I informed the principal, quoting my father. "And more than a dozen harmless ones in our part of the state." The principal was unmoved.

I began bringing home garter snakes that showed up in the garden and water snakes from the nearby brook. I scooped up eggs from the water and watched them hatch into tadpoles and salamanders. Father built cages for our hamsters and rabbits. Two turtles that Ruth named Attila the Hun and Alaric the Visigoth lived under the piano. We no longer had a dog. Sadly, Rover had been carried off by old age a year earlier.

On my birthday Father surprised me with a baby boa constrictor. She was beautiful, cream-colored with reddish-brown markings, and she twisted herself around my wrist like a bracelet. I called her Cleopatra.

Ruth said, "That name makes no sense."

"It does to me," I snapped. "It is the snake the Egyptian queen used to kill herself."

"That was an asp," Ruth argued. "Not a boa."

My interest turned to butterflies. I gathered dozens of them and put them in drinking glasses arranged upside down in rows on the windowsills. For weeks I put leaves in their glass cages, and not just any leaf but only the kind that type of butterfly laid its eggs on. Eventually, some of the caterpillars entered the next stage, the chrysalis.

"This is where the metamorphosis happens," Father explained. "Now you must wait. And watch."

Father planned to take photographs with his old-fashioned camera. He set up his tripod, opened the camera with the accordion-shaped bellows perched on it, inserted the glass plates, and focused the lens. One by one the chrysalises began to burst open, and each damp shape emerged and spread its beautiful butterfly wings. Father clicked the shutter.

"Let me look," I begged. He stepped aside while I ducked my head under the black camera cloth and peered into the viewfinder. The image was upside down. Better not to have the camera in the way, I thought. Better just to *look*.

Afterward, he closed himself in the bathroom in total darkness, bathed the glass plates in separate trays of awful-smelling chemicals, rinsed them, and set them up to dry. He printed the best of the glass negatives on special paper, another messy process. Father's photographs hung on the walls in every room of our house—pictures of Mother draped in a shawl, of us children, of the flowers in our garden and the birds that visited there. I helped him choose which chrysalis-to-butterfly pictures to hang.

Mainly, though, Father *thought*. Once he took our family to a restaurant for dinner, a rare treat, and just as our food arrived, an idea came to him. He began to sketch a diagram on the tablecloth. We ate, and he drew. Ruth and I nudged each other, wondering when he would notice the fried chicken growing cold on his plate. He left without eating a single bite.

"Are you going to take the tablecloth, Father?" Roger asked, startling him out of his thought cloud.

Father shook his head, tapping his forehead. "Unnecessary. I have it here."

Mother grew impatient with him. "If only he would talk more!" she complained. He was a brilliant inventor, she said, and his ideas made his bosses rich. Mother tried to get him to ask for a raise in pay, but Father didn't seem to care much about that.

◆◆

In grammar school Tubby's mother bought her dresses in gay colors with ruffles and lace that I envied, but Mother would have none of it. She dressed me in dark-colored skirts and white middy blouses with sailor collars. "Very practical for everyday," she said.

My hair was parted in the middle and pulled back in plaits. Ruth was supposed to braid my hair every morning, and if she and I had argued about something, she punished me by pulling them so tight that I couldn't blink. Mother said I could do away with braids when I reached high school. But not a word about dresses.

Mother signed Ruth and me up for dancing classes because, she promised, "If you dance well, you will never lack for partners."

The boys in the class, sent by their anxious mothers, obviously wanted to be anywhere else. The teacher paired us off according to height, and her assistant banged out a peppy tune on the piano. Short, shy partners steered me glumly around the polished floor. Later, at home, I danced by myself, dreaming of the day some boy would actually ask me to dance.

Each year the grammar school held four dances for the seventh and eighth graders. I came down with a cold and missed the autumn affair, but after weeks of dancing classes I was primed for the Christmas party. Teachers would chaperone, and parents volunteered refreshments. I asked Mother if we could contribute cookies.

"If you wish to take cookies, you must bake them yourself. You certainly know how."

I wanted to take something that would be *different*. Suddenly inspired, I decided to forget baking cookies and take pickles instead. I loved Grandmother White's dill pickles. My mother did not care for them. The jar had sat unopened in the cupboard for a very long time.

The night of the Christmas dance I put on my dark green dress-up dress, high-top shoes, and the dreadful cotton stockings and set off with the jar of pickles.

I put my contribution on the table decorated with jolly Santa Clauses, among an array of tiny tarts, fancy cakes, cookies in the shape of Christmas trees. Some thought the pickles were a joke; others weren't so sure, but no one wanted to sample any of Grandmother White's sour dills. I made a show of eating three of them myself.

Not a single boy asked me to dance. They asked other girls—

even Tubby got asked, although it was by a boy she couldn't stand.

I dumped the rest of the pickles behind a bush on the way home and reported to Mother that it was a very nice party. Secretly I wept.

And I told Ruth the truth. I always told my sister the truth.

"Pickles?" Ruth exclaimed. "You took a *jar of pickles* to the dance? Why on earth did you do that?"

"I didn't want to be like everybody else," I mumbled.

"Well, I guess you succeeded." Ruth sat down beside me on my bed and put her arm around my shoulders. "Boys your age are not at their best. You're probably smarter than all of them, so they stay away from you. That will change as you get older. One of these days—and it's coming soon, I promise you—the boys will be standing in line for a chance to dance with you. But," she added, "you probably didn't help your case by taking pickles."

2

Plainfield High School—1917

RUTH WAS A JUNIOR WHEN I ENTERED PLAINFIELD High School as a freshman. She made sure I knew all about the social divisions at the school. There was the "crystal-chandelier set," snobbish girls who shopped for stylish clothes in New York City and attended lots of parties. Then there were the "linsey-woolseys." Linsey-woolsey was cloth woven from a mixture of linen and wool, plain and serviceable. Ruth and I were linsey-woolseys.

Mother made all of our clothes and taught us to sew. "It will come in handy someday," she promised. I took to it eagerly. I believed that, if I got good enough, I could eventually make myself the kind of stylish clothes I wanted. The kind I felt I deserved.

"You are not pretty, Margaret," my mother told me frankly—she never attempted to soften her words—"but you have an interesting face."

My dark, deep-set eyes were like my father's, but my face, like his, was a little too round. I had Mother's thick, dark hair, but my lips were a little too thin, like hers. An interesting face.

I did not want to have an interesting face. Crystal-chandelier girls had pretty faces, not interesting ones.

I had already made up my mind that I would be famous, and rich, too, and the crystal-chandelier girls as well as the linsey-woolseys would look back at their high-school yearbook and marvel at what had become of Peggy White. The one with the interesting face.

Boys seemed to like me well enough. They invited me to paddle canoes on the Raritan River and to go on hikes, because I wasn't afraid of anything, not deep water or high places. I could identify plants and birdcalls. I was fourteen years old, but none of the boys who asked me if a snake was poisonous ever asked me to dance.

◆◆

In my sophomore year—Ruth was a senior, getting ready to graduate—I heard about a writing contest. The Babcock Prize was being offered for "excellence in literary composition," an eight-hundred-word short story to be finished by the end of the semester, in June. The prize was fifteen dollars' worth of books to be chosen by the winner. Sophomores were eligible to enter, but no sophomore had ever won, and everyone understood that the prize would go to a junior or senior. I would not have to take the usual English exams if I entered the contest.

I informed my English teacher, Miss Aubrey, of my plans. "I know you'll do well, Margaret," she said. "You've shown that you have talent. But remember that you must never leave a task until you've completed it to the best of your ability." She sounded just like my mother.

I put the whole thing out of my mind. There was plenty of time to think of an idea for a short story. The end of the semester was still a long way off.

Spring came, and the weather warmed. Others in my class had to sit through dreary exams; I did not. I was writing a short story, or would be quite soon. And then, suddenly, the last day of school was *the next day*. The story had to be delivered to the front porch of the principal's house by half past five, and I didn't have even the germ of an idea.

At lunchtime, Tubby and I sat on a mossy stone wall near the school, eating our sandwiches. "What am I going to do, Tubby?" I wailed. "If I don't hand in a story, Miss Aubrey will fail me. I told her I was entering the contest, and I will have let her down."

"You're going to write a story, of course," Tubby said.

"I don't have an idea in my head," I moaned. "I haven't even thought about it."

"You're going to start thinking right now." She began to peel the orange in her lunchbox. "A dog story," she said, and closed her eyes as if she were having a vision. "Everybody loves dog stories."

I thought about our dog, Rover. I'd been yearning for another dog ever since Rover died, but I had not persuaded my parents that we should have one.

The bell rang. I had algebra and geography classes before dismissal. "Meet me in the library at three o'clock," I told Tubby. "I'll come up with an idea by then."

For the next hour I was not thinking about quadratic equations and coefficients. I was doodling possible dog names on my algebra worksheet. By the end of class, I had settled on Sparky, an abandoned mutt yearning for a home. While the geography teacher droned on about major river systems, I worked on a name for the boy and decided to call him Rob, an unhappy little boy yearning for a dog.

After dismissal Tubby and I retreated to a corner of the library. "I have an idea," I whispered to Tubby. "Here's how we'll do it. I'll write a page, and while I'm working on the next part, you check my grammar and spelling and count the number of words."

The yellow dog was tired and hungry, I scribbled, *and also very dirty.* I read my first sentence. *Was,* I decided, was a weak verb. I scratched it out. *The dog trotted wearily down the dark alley, searching for something—anything—to eat. Burrs matted his filthy yellow fur.* My pencil raced across the page. I introduced Rob, whose father was a sea captain away on a voyage to Africa. Mama, stern but loving, told poor Rob that he could not have a dog.

I handed the first page over to Tubby and tried not to look at the clock.

"Two hundred words on page one," she announced. "You need three more pages."

At four o'clock the library closed, and we moved outside to the stone wall.

Sparky spotted a lonely-looking boy, wagged his tail, and gazed at the boy pleadingly. The boy took the pup home. But Mama said harshly, "Get that flea-ridden mutt out of here." Rob watched tearfully as Sparky slunk away.

But Rob continued to feed Sparky in secret.

"Three hundred and eighty-five," Tubby announced.

By four-thirty I was within a hundred and twenty words of the end. The captain returned from his voyage, and Sparky greeted him so joyously that Mama declared that the dog must become a member of the family.

Tubby didn't believe the ending. "Why would Mama change her mind so suddenly?"

I rewrote that part. Sparky barked his head off when the captain returned. Impressed, the captain persuaded Mama the mutt was exactly what she needed as a watchdog. Done!

The two of us raced to the principal's house and added my masterpiece to the pile on the front porch. I had no hope of winning, but at least I would not fail my English class and disappoint Miss Aubrey.

A week later the winner was announced: *I had won!* This was even more unlikely than a happy ending for Sparky. The prize would be awarded at commencement exercises. I already knew exactly which books I wanted: *The Frog Book*, *The Moth Book*, and *The Reptile Book*.

Tubby was thrilled for me; Ruth was, too. "There's a dance after the commencement exercises," she reminded me. "Mother and I are making me a new dress."

Of course I knew about the dance! I was almost fifteen, and I had spent my entire school career as a wallflower, but I truly believed that winning the writing contest was about to change everything. Every boy at Plainfield High School would recognize this literary Cinderella and want to dance with her.

Mother agreed that I, too, needed a new dress, and her sewing machine chattered far into the night to finish it in time.

Commencement took place on a warm June evening in the school auditorium. I had not only a new dress—maroon with a white linen collar and cuffs—but also new shoes. At least our cotton stockings were white instead of black. The graduating class, solemn in royal blue caps and gowns, took seats in the front rows. Behind them were juniors who were receiving prizes, and one sophomore—me. The orchestra played, a local minister offered an opening prayer, followed by a piano solo, and several speeches.

I was in a delicious froth of excitement when the principal appeared at the podium carrying a bundle of fat green books tied with white ribbons. "Miss Margaret White, please step forward to receive the Babcock Award!"

I climbed onto the stage and waited as the principal spoke of the "fresh, young talent discovered in the person of Miss Margaret White, not yet fifteen years of age, whose short story 'Rob and Sparky' shows how much we have to look forward to as Miss White makes her way into the future as a writer." He transferred the tomes to my arms, the audience politely applauded, and I returned to my seat, beaming.

The graduating seniors filed up to the stage to receive their diplomas. The commencement exercises ended, chairs were folded and stacked, and potted palms were carried in from the hall to transform the auditorium into a ballroom.

The Aristocrats, a five-piece band, had been hired for the evening, and as the lights were lowered, they began to play "I'm Forever Blowing Bubbles." Couples drifted out to the center of the ballroom. I stood on the sidelines, clutching my bundle of books, sure that at any minute one of the boys in my class, or possibly even an upperclassman, would recognize that I was *a star*. I had won the Babcock Prize!

The Aristocrats launched into "A Pretty Girl Is Like a Melody." Even Tubby had a partner, a myopic boy with thick glasses. A stag line had formed, and a few boys stepped out boldly and cut in on the dancing couples. The new partner swept off with the girl in his arms, and her former partner joined the stag line. One of those boys might glance my way and ask me to dance, but none did.

There was still plenty of time. The dance floor had become crowded. The violinist took up a waltz. I loved to waltz, but nobody even looked in my direction. The bundle of books in my arms grew heavier, and so did my heart.

Out of the crowd stepped Stella, a friend of Ruth's. Stella, five feet eleven and a half, who might have qualified as a crystal-chandelier girl if she hadn't been quite so tall, noticed me standing there alone and walked over to me.

"Peggy," said Stella warmly, "congratulations on winning the Babcock! What an honor! This is something worth celebrating, isn't it? Ruth's already left, I believe, but she's been telling me that you're a swell dancer. Come on, let's get out there and show them some of your fancy steps."

What utter humiliation! I tried to think of an excuse, but Stella didn't wait for an answer. "Here, I'll put those books somewhere," she said. She deposited them behind a potted palm, seized my hand, and whirled me onto the dance floor. The piano thumped out "A Good Man Is Hard to Find," and I would have given anything to disappear.

3

A Glorious Future—1919

AFTER THAT TORTURED EVENING, I MOPED AROUND SO
much that my two friends decided to do something.

"We have a surprise for you," Sara Jane announced. It was
the thirteenth of June, the day before I would turn fifteen. "As a
birthday gift, Tubby and I are taking you to New York, to visit Miss
Jessie Fowler of the American Phrenology Institute."

I knew about phrenology. An expert could feel the bumps on
your head and analyze your personality, point out your strengths
and weaknesses, and guide you in your future choices. I was
skeptical, but it sounded like an adventure.

Assuring Mother that we'd come straight home afterward,
the three of us, in our hats and gloves, boarded the local train
for the city. The sun baked the sidewalks as we made our way
to a building on Broadway near 36th Street. We stopped to look
in a show window with a display of bald china heads. A map of
the organs of the mind was drawn on each head. A receptionist
directed us to a parlor crowded with uncomfortable furniture.
Nervous and excited, we waited.

At last we were led to Miss Fowler's private office. Heavy

velvet draperies blocked off all natural light. The only illumination came from a small desk lamp with a green shade. The lady behind the large carved desk was dressed in a black suit and a white blouse. Her gray hair struggled to escape from the severe bun at the nape of her neck. She glanced at the three of us, and her gaze came to rest on my head. I was wearing a large blue straw hat, loaned to me by my sister.

"Miss White, you are here for a consultation?" I nodded. "Kindly remove your hat." She pointed to a chair beside her desk. Sara Jane and Tubby retreated to a settee against the wall.

Eyes closed, Miss Fowler stood before me and ran practiced hands around my temples, up my forehead and across my skull, then down the sides around my ears. She did not speak. I sat perfectly still, staring at the lace jabot cascading over her ample bosom. When she had finished her examination, she settled at her desk and made notes on a large sheet of paper printed with a silhouette outline of a head marked into sections and labeled: Language, for example, was located at the eye; Memory, on the forehead, close to Agreeableness.

"Very well, Miss White, I imagine you are quite eager to hear the results of the examination."

"Yes, ma'am."

Miss Fowler regarded me with pale blue eyes. "You have a most interesting cranium," she said. "Your head measures a little above the average. It's twenty-one and three-quarter inches in circumference, and the average is twenty-one and one-half. You show a fair balance of power between body and brain. I see that you are eager and adventuresome, prepared to travel to any destination to gather information on whatever topic interests you, regardless of the difficulties you may encounter. I believe that you would benefit greatly from world travel. I advise you to take photographs of the places you visit and the sights you see, in order to give lectures about your adventures to your friends and family when you return."

There was more: possible focuses for my energy and talent in the fields of music, childhood diseases, even home decoration. All this deduced from the shape of my head!

Tubby and Sara Jane paid Miss Fowler with their pooled funds—I would have paid her double had she asked for it—and we stepped into the dazzling sunlight, talking of practically nothing else as we waited for the train back to Bound Brook. I may have been a wallflower at the commencement dance, and at every dance I'd attended before it, but now I had Miss Fowler's assurance and my own belief that the bumps on my head indicated a glorious future in which I would truly be a star, whatever I chose to do.

4

Her Glorious Fancies—1919

MY GLORIOUS FUTURE WAS A LONG WAY OFF. Meanwhile, I desperately wanted to fit in somewhere; I just didn't know where. Finally at the start of my junior year I joined the debating society.

One of the questions being debated that fall was, *Should women be granted the right to vote?* Congress had finally passed a law granting women's suffrage, but thirty-six states had to vote in favor of making the law an amendment to the Constitution. New Jersey had not yet voted.

"I hope you're taking the negative side in the debate," said Mother.

This came as a surprise—I knew she was wholeheartedly in favor of women voting. "Surely you don't think I'm opposed!"

"Of course you're not!" she snapped. "But for you to take the side you agree with would be a mistake. That's the easy side! Remember, Margaret, always choose the harder path."

That was how I wound up in a room full of people, arguing for something I didn't believe—that women should *not* be allowed to vote. "Because it's the proper role of men to protect women,"

I declared, "and because women are by their nature unable to protect themselves, men must continue to exercise this solemn duty. Since voters have the duty to serve on juries, and since jurors sometimes hear descriptions of deplorable acts, women must be kept off juries."

I looked out at my audience. They were hanging on every word. "Furthermore," I argued, "allowing the weaker sex to take part in political discussions could upset the harmony of the home, and allowing women to run for public office could pit one woman against another, a situation distressing to civilized society."

None of these were my ideas. I found them in an anti-suffragist pamphlet and tried to translate the arrogant nonsense into something that sounded like my own words. But I argued so logically and convincingly that I won the debate. Afterward I felt guilty—what if I had actually persuaded someone to that way of thinking?

The boy who had argued in favor of women having the right to vote invited me to go out for a soda afterward, so that he could talk some sense into my misguided head. I let him think he had persuaded me. He seemed very pleased with himself.

In February of 1920, New Jersey became the twenty-ninth state to vote in favor of the amendment.

◆◆

That spring the drama club announced plans to put on two short plays: *Rosalie*, a three-character melodrama, and *The Bluffers*, a revue with a dozen or so characters. Both plays were set in France. Despite my complete lack of stage experience, I tried out for the title role of Rosalie, the maid, and was picked for the part. Violet-eyed Eleanor Treacy, leader of the crystal-chandelier set, was cast as Madame Bol. The role of Monsieur Bol went to Charley Drayton, the handsomest boy in our class. I liked Charley a *lot*, but he went out with crystal-chandelier girls and naturally was not interested in a linsey-woolsey. I didn't know if Charley and Eleanor were going out together, but they flirted constantly.

"Coming to the cast party?" Eleanor asked after the Saturday night performance. I was wiping off my stage makeup with cold cream, and Eleanor was skillfully applying rouge and lipstick, neither of which I was permitted to wear. "It's at Charley's house," she said, moving on to eyebrow pencil. "All the *Bluffer* boys will be there, and the stage crew, too. There'll be lots to eat, and dancing, too, of course." Eye shadow was next.

"Sorry, but I can't," I said. "I already have other plans."

"Oh, too bad," said Eleanor, but I felt sure she wasn't at all disappointed. My "other plans" were a fabrication, but I'd decided that the best way to avoid being humiliated at a dance was not to attend one.

◆◆

At the start of my senior year I signed up to work on the staff of *The Oracle*, the school's monthly magazine. Charley Drayton was the editor-in-chief. He had an ingratiating manner and an easy grin, but he was also lazy, and the rest of us had to take up the slack for him, which we performed gladly at the time and then resented later when he got most of the credit. My title was School Editor, and my job was to edit articles about student activities. Mary Nancy Paluso, a linsey-woolsey nicknamed Mimsy, was the literary editor overseeing short stories and poetry, an assignment I would have preferred.

The final issue of the year was published as the class yearbook, with individual photographs of the graduating seniors along with each person's nickname, ambition, list of activities during their four years of high school, and a classical quotation that was supposed to reflect the senior's personality. Brainy Mimsy, of course, came up with the quotations.

Tubby's was from a poem by Alfred, Lord Tennyson, "A Dream of Fair Women": *A daughter of the gods, divinely tall, / And most divinely fair.* Mine was from a poem by James Russell Lowell, "My Love": *Her glorious fancies come from far, / Beneath the silver evening-star, / And yet her heart is ever near.*

"'Glorious fancies,'" said Tubby. "Just like Miss Fowler predicted."

Jean Runyon was in charge of gathering the information on each graduating senior. We went over it together, checking spelling and punctuation.

Margaret B. White. (The B was for Bourke; my mother had given me her maiden name as my middle name.) *Nickname: Peggy. Ambition: Herpetologist.*

"Herpetologist?" Jean asked. "What's that?"

"Someone who studies reptiles and amphibians," I explained. "Snakes, mostly, but also frogs and toads, newts, salamanders. And also lizards and turtles. They're all herps."

Jean shuddered. "I remember the time you came to school with a snake wrapped around each arm. And back in eighth grade, when you brought a snake to school and all the girls screamed, and the boys put on a show of not being scared, but I knew they were."

"I didn't want to scare anybody. The snake wasn't poisonous. I just thought it was interesting."

"Maybe." She shuffled through the forms she'd collected. "Other girls want to be teachers, and a couple say they want to be nurses, but I know that Dottie Hendricks, for instance, gets sick to her stomach when something doesn't smell right. Eleanor Treacy says she's planning to study art and become an illustrator. Most of them, though, just want to get married. The boys hope to go to sea or become doctors. But so far you're the only one who wants to be anything like a herpetologist." She arranged the papers in a neat stack. "What would you actually do with those creepy, scaly things?"

"I'll visit dark and interesting jungles and collect specimens for natural history museums. I'll learn so much about them that people will invite me to give lectures. Maybe I'll become a famous scientist, and then I'll marry a famous scientist, another herpetologist, and we'll travel all over the world together."

"You really want to do that? That's kind of a strange thing for a girl to do."

"I want to do all kinds of things that girls never do. That *women* never do. Didn't you ever think of doing something like that?"

Jean looked at me skeptically. "I just want to go to normal school and earn my teaching certificate, because my dad wants me to, and teach for two years while Tom finishes his degree, and then we'll get married."

We went back to checking the seniors' forms. My list of activities was among the longest in the class—decorating committees, ice cream receptions, pageants, swim team, class secretary. I added another one: class song.

Along with pimply Jack Daniels I was elected by the staff of *The Oracle* to write the words to the class song. It would be sung at commencement to the tune of the Plainfield High School alma mater.

I'd been writing poetry since I was a child. Mother kept most of my early scribblings in a box, along with my report cards, beginning in first grade. "Just look at this," my mother had said the last time she'd added something to my box, and pulled out a crumpled bit of paper with my handwriting. "'Flit on, lovely butterfly / Into a world more fair / With azure sky far more high / Than that blue sky up there.' You wrote that when you were eleven—see, I put the date on it: August 1915."

Now I sat in the library across from Jack Daniels, trying to come up with an idea for the song. I didn't much care for Jack. He'd already had his poetry published in some little magazine no one had heard of, and he seemed overly impressed with his own brilliance.

"We have to work the class colors into the poem," Jack said. "That's a good place to start."

"I didn't know we even *had* class colors. What are they?"

Jack looked at me with disdain. "For your information, they're red and gray, and we voted on them last fall, before the Autumn Festival dance. You don't recall that?"

"But aren't there some *other* school colors? Scarlet and azure?"

"Red and blue, Peg," Jack sighed. "Red and blue are the *school* colors. We're talking now about our *class* colors."

I once wrote an eight-hundred-word short story with less fuss, but after hours of discussion, we cobbled together a poem.

Our Red and Gray we'll ne'er forget, / We'll always to our Class be true. / What e'er we do throughout our lives / We'll keep unstained the Red and Blue.

"Very colorful," I allowed.

I graduated in June with high grades and plans to attend Barnard College in New York City. Mimsy was the valedictorian, no surprise, and gave a stirring address on "Beauty in Modern Life" with references to art, music, poetry, and dance. Prizes were awarded in Latin, physics, chemistry, and mathematics, and Mimsy collected the Babcock Prize for her short story based on Hermione, the daughter of Helen of Troy. "I didn't even know Helen had a daughter," Tubby said. "But if anybody would know, it's Mimsy."

That summer I took the train to New Brunswick, where I enrolled in classes in swimming and aesthetic dancing at Rutgers

University. I was already a good swimmer, but I wanted to become an *excellent* swimmer. As a herpetologist collecting specimens in the wild, I might frequently be around bodies of water. The Amazon, maybe, or the Nile!

I had learned the waltz and the foxtrot in dancing class, but aesthetic dancing was a form of self-expression that didn't require a partner. The instructor was a gaunt woman in a flowing black skirt, her dark hair with a dramatic white streak worn in a chignon.

"Focus on the center of your body," she told us. "Concentrate on your breathing and how you move. Breathe! Move! Feel that energy coursing through your entire body!"

Day after day I breathed and I moved. I had always been a bit chubby, but the swimming and dancing streamlined my body. One of the dancers loaned me a lipstick and showed me how to use it. I looked in the mirror and liked what I saw. No longer a plain, baby-faced girl but a pretty seventeen-year-old smiled back at me.

The other thing that happened that summer was my growing friendship with our well-to-do neighbors, Mr. Henry Munger and his sister, Miss Jessie Munger, who lived a few blocks away. Bound Brook was not a wealthy town. The Mungers could have lived in nearby Plainfield, a town of large villas, sweeping green lawns, and elaborate flowerbeds, but for some reason they chose not to. Mr. Munger puttered around his flowers and looked after his own grass, although he had reached an age when that was becoming harder. Sometimes my mother sent Roger over to the Mungers' to help out. They always tried to pay Roger, but Mother forbade him to accept any money.

"It's what neighbors *do*," she said. "They look out for each other."

Roger objected, saying he wanted to have some extra

spending money, and he promised to save half of whatever he made, but Mother was unbending. So Roger rode over on his bicycle to help with the weeding and mowing in summer and snow shoveling in winter and sometimes ran errands for Miss Munger. She probably slipped him a quarter every now and then and Roger didn't say no, but he didn't tell Mother.

Miss Munger had problems with her eyesight, and two or three times a week I read to her for an hour or so. Between chapters Miss Munger called for tea, and as though he were a servant, Mr. Munger carried in a large silver tray and a plate of slightly stale cookies. When I told Mother, she began sending over a tin of cookies fresh from our oven.

Miss Munger was fond of historical novels set in England and featuring the Tudors. She loved every one of Henry VIII's wives. She was interested in many other things as well, and I once brought my hognose snake to visit. Miss Munger squinted at him when he reared up and hissed at her and applauded softly when he played dead.

"What is it you intend to study, Margaret?" she asked on my last visit before I was to leave for college.

"Herpetology."

"The study of snakes! How thrilling!" she said. "But is that a proper calling for a young lady? Still, one does sometimes wish for the unusual, doesn't one!" Then she added thoughtfully that the highlight of her life had been a trip to India with her grandmother when she was a girl. "I remember the snake charmer playing his pungi, and the cobra rising up out of his basket. How exciting for you!"

◆◆

I was packing my clothes, folding another drab dress as well as several pairs of those awful cotton stockings. Ruth, home from college in Boston, sat on her bed, across from mine, and assured me that from now on everything would be different.

"College boys aren't like those boys who didn't pay attention to you in high school," she said. "You probably scared them off. You're too smart, too ambitious, too *driven*. Boys that age don't know what to make of a girl like you. But that will change. You'll see."

"Has it changed for you?" I asked. It didn't seem to me that much had. She was still wearing cotton stockings and the dresses she'd made herself in high school.

"I'm not like you, Peg," Ruth replied. "I love the law classes I'm taking, I get good grades, and I'm contented with that. I don't want to be different. And you *do*."

"Yes," I said. "That's true."

When I'd finished packing, we all piled into the family car, and Father drove to the dormitory at Barnard. Columbia University didn't admit women, but I could enroll in science courses there and take my other required courses at Barnard, the women's college on the opposite side of Broadway.

Father set down the battered old suitcase Mother had loaned me. "Call if you need anything." That was all he said, but I thought his eyes looked watery. I know mine were.

"Remember, Margaret, never take the easy way," Mother said, predictably.

Roger promised to take care of my various animals.

They got back in the car, and I watched them drive away. I picked up the suitcase and walked toward Brooks Hall with its row of Greek columns.

From now on everything will be different, Ruth had promised. I hoped she was right.

5

A Mature and Intelligent Young Woman—1921

I'D SIGNED UP FOR BIOLOGY, BOTANY, MATHEMATICS, and chemistry at Columbia. Most of the students in my classes were boys. They ignored me. The girls in my residence hall laughed at things I didn't find funny, and they never seemed to tire of discussing clothes and parties and the handsome philosophy professor. My roommate, Madge Jacobson, a pretty girl with a curly blond bob and a closetful of smart dresses, would have fit in perfectly with the crystal-chandeliers. While I was studying in the library, Madge and her friends spent their free time playing bridge and drinking coffee. Madge had an infectious laugh and always seemed ready to have fun, and she didn't mind that I kept a couple of pet snakes in a terrarium next to my desk.

We had strict curfews—eight o'clock on weeknights, midnight on weekends. The curfews didn't bother me. Why would I want to stay out any later? There was a telephone in a booth at the end of the hall, and we had to take turns answering with, "Good evening, Fourth Floor Brooks Hall," from seven until quiet hours began at ten; no calls were allowed after ten. I hated that one hour a week when it was my turn to sit by the phone. It never rang for me, except when Mother called every other Sunday.

At the start of Christmas vacation I caught the train to Bound Brook. I had brought along a satchel of books, and I was deep in a chapter on cycloalkanes when a male voice asked if the seat next to me was available. I glanced up and nodded. He was tall and thin with fine features and bright blue eyes behind horn-rimmed glasses that slipped down his nose. He looked older. He observed me observing him and pointed to the book in my lap.

"Organic chemistry," he said. "You're a student, then?"

"Columbia University. I plan to major in herpetology."

He was on his way to a chemical factory in Bound Brook where he was about to start work as a research chemist. "They manufacture dyes," he said. He held out his hand. "My name is François Gilfillan, but please call me Gil."

"Peggy White," I said, shaking his hand. "My home is in Bound Brook."

"I'm from Ninnekah, Oklahoma," he said.

We got off the train at Bound Brook. My father had come to meet me, and I introduced him to Gil.

"It appears that your daughter and I have similar interests in science, Mr. White," Gil said. "May I have your permission to call her?"

Father glanced at me, and a little smile twitched at his lips. "Of course, Mr. Gilfillan," he said.

Gil did call two days later. At Mother's suggestion, I invited him to come for Christmas dinner, and he accepted.

My parents didn't practice any religion, so there was no decorated tree, no wreath on the front door. My parents saw no reason for shiny glass balls or holly. If Ruth hadn't persuaded Mother to buy a big roasting chicken, she would have probably served our usual Sunday menu—chicken fricassee and dumplings. Besides the chicken, we would have mashed potatoes, glazed carrots, and Parker House rolls. "For dessert we'll have apple pie à la mode," Ruth said. "I'll make it."

"'Pie à la mode!'" Mother sniffed. "You've been spending too much time with the upper crust in Boston." Ruth didn't bother to reply.

Mother and Ruth and I spent Christmas morning in the kitchen. After everything was prepared, I went upstairs to change. I wished I had something festive to wear—everything I owned seemed just the opposite—but I did have the tube of dark red lipstick I'd purchased last summer. When I came downstairs, Mother saw me and frowned. "It makes you look cheap, Margaret," she said, but she did not send me to the bathroom to wipe it off.

Gil arrived, cheeks reddened with cold, wishing everyone a merry Christmas and presenting Mother with a box of chocolates. Gil and Father hit it off immediately, as I expected they would. While I was mashing the potatoes, Father was asking Gil questions. "So, Gil, where do you hail from?"

"Well, sir, I was born in Oklahoma," I heard Gil say, "and my family moved to Texas when I was a boy. Then I went to visit an uncle in Oregon and wound up getting a degree in pharmacy there before I joined the army."

He talked about where he'd served during the great war against Germany, and how, after his discharge, he'd gone to Yale and earned a doctorate in chemistry. "Now I'm at Calco Chemical as a research chemist."

Mother set a bowl of gravy on the table. "And how old did you say you are, Mr. Gilfillan?"

"Twenty-eight, Mrs. White. I'll be twenty-nine next month."

"Twenty-eight!" Mother sounded shocked. "Are you aware that Margaret is just seventeen?"

I was a bit shocked, too, but Gil answered smoothly, "Peg—Margaret—strikes me as a very mature and intelligent young woman."

A bright little bubble of happiness expanded in my chest. Not a seventeen-year-old girl—*a mature and intelligent young woman*! I bit my lip to hide a grin.

Ruth announced that dinner was served. Father carved inexpertly, as though he'd never seen a whole roast chicken, and the side dishes were passed around. It was a quiet meal. Father didn't like a lot of conversation when we were at the table.

We hardly ever had guests for dinner, and none of us knew how to act. Roger stared at Gil with undisguised curiosity. "You must be pretty important," he said. "We never eat like this."

"I'll take that as a compliment," Gil said easily, and accepted more mashed potatoes.

I jumped up to carry dirty dishes to the kitchen and stayed to scrape them, glad for something to do.

"You should be in there entertaining your beau," Mother whispered when she brought out the skeleton of the chicken. "Goodness knows your father won't do it."

"He's not my beau! And he and Father are actually talking." We could hear the murmur of conversation, and I relaxed a little.

Ruth served her apple pie à la mode, and Roger announced that he had cranked the ice cream freezer himself. My parents didn't drink coffee, so they didn't offer any. We sat on and on at the table, trying to think of something to say, until Roger spoke up again. "Do you want to see my rabbits?"

We trooped out to the backyard. Roger introduced his bunnies and allowed Gil to pet them. But when it began to snow lightly, Gil praised the meal one more time, wished us a happy Christmas again, shook hands with Father, and retrieved his hat and overcoat.

"Good-bye, Peggy," he said. "Thank you for inviting me to be a part of your family's celebration."

Celebration? It hadn't seemed like much of a celebration. Gil stepped out into the whirling snow. I watched from the window. He shoved his hands deep in his pockets, hurried down the front walk, and turned the corner.

"Well," said Mother, dropping into her chair. "That's that."

◆◆

Gil telephoned me at Brooks Hall—the first phone call I'd received there, other than from my mother—and invited me to have dinner with him on January 12, his birthday. He would take the train into the city after work. "We can meet at Pierre's. It's a little French restaurant near the train station."

When I told Madge that I planned to wear my one good dress, she offered to loan me an entire outfit. "You're going to Pierre's, my dear," she said. "You must dress up for the occasion."

Out came Madge's smart black suit, peacock-blue hat and gloves, and silk stockings—the stockings alone made me feel as though I was dressed to the nines. My tweed coat would have to do. Mother had bought it for me when I was a freshman in high school, a larger size than I usually wore because she thought I hadn't finished growing. It was still at least one size too big.

"Now the makeup," Madge said, and went to work—rouge on the cheeks, powder on the nose, black pencil around the eyes, and finally my dark red lipstick. "Remember to redo the lipstick when you've finished eating. Be sure to blot your lips, and be careful when he kisses you that you don't smudge," she warned.

When he kisses me? I hadn't considered that possibility. The girls in our wing of the residence hall had thoroughly discussed when it was proper to let a boy kiss you the first time. Most agreed on the third date. A few fast ones dismissed this as prudish. "If you want to kiss him on the first date, then do it! What's the harm in that?"

"But you want the boy to respect you," argued unattractive

Muriel, and the prudes nodded sagely.

Madge sided with the fast girls. "Kissing is fine, but no petting," Madge said. "Not until you've been going out together regularly for a couple of months."

I'd listened, not wanting to admit that I didn't know what petting was. When I asked later, back in our room, Madge explained, "No touching below the neck." The other girls seemed to have had plenty of experience—or talked as though they did—and had established timetables for each step beyond the first kiss. But this would be my first real date. I was sure that Gil must have had plenty of dates and would know what was expected. He didn't seem like the type to take advantage of a girl.

I checked the seams on my borrowed stockings one more time. "Are they straight?" I asked Madge. "Is my slip showing?"

"Relax," Madge said. "You're fine. Have fun."

I arrived at Pierre's too early. Not sure what a girl was supposed to do while waiting, I ordered coffee, even though I never drank it, but I felt that ordering a glass of milk would betray my inexperience. The waiter appeared indifferent. I poured in as much cream as the cup would hold and sipped the pale coffee. Should I pay for it? Or wait for Gil to do it?

· He rushed in, overcoat flapping, glasses steaming in the sudden heat of the restaurant, full of apologies and explanations: his boss wanted additional data before he could leave. He slid into a chair across from me. "Well," he said, smiling, "here we are."

"Happy birthday," I said. *Should I have bought him a gift? But what would have been the right thing to buy?*

"Thank you."

Could Gil see how nervous I was? I'd left a red lipstick print on the rim of the coffee cup. Should I go to the ladies room and put on more? Or wait until after I'd eaten?

Before I could decide, the waiter brought menus. "*Bonsoir,* m'sieur et mam'selle," he said with a stiff bow. I recognized a few words, but when the waiter recommended the *coq au vin*, whatever it was, I took his suggestion.

Gil talked about his work in the lab and asked questions about herpetology that sounded as though he wasn't just being polite. Boys in high school had fled when the conversation veered toward my future—like traveling and bringing back live specimens and giving lectures—but Gil paid attention. By the time I'd finished my chicken in wine sauce, my self-consciousness had almost disappeared.

We'd barely finished our *mousse au chocolat* when we realized we'd have to rush to make it to the residence hall by curfew. Gil took my elbow and hustled me across streets and along sidewalks to the entry of Brooks Hall. There was no time to even *think* about a kiss. I stepped into the brightly lit lobby, past the housemother frowning at her watch.

For five days I thought often of Gil, wondering if there would be another date and another possibility for a kiss. At last, I received a telephone call. But it wasn't Gil. It was Mother.

"Come home as quick as you can, Margaret. Father is in a coma."

6

MY FATHER HAD SUFFERED A STROKE. IT WAS NOT his first.

The first stroke had happened five years earlier, when I was twelve and in the eighth grade. We'd just finished supper. It was Ruth's turn to wash the dishes; I was drying. Father sat in his usual chair, thinking, and Mother sat in her chair, sewing and probably trying to get him to talk to her. He made an odd noise and slumped over. Mother jumped up and ran to him. He tried to talk, but made only strange garbled sounds. Ruth rushed to call the doctor.

It was a stroke, the doctor told us then. Father could not move his left arm or leg, part of his face was paralyzed, and he couldn't speak. I thought he was going to die. But he didn't, and every day as soon as school was out, I sat beside him and talked.

Mr. Hoe, the owner of the company where Father worked, came to visit him. "We are much indebted to you, White," I remember Mr. Hoe saying, patting my father's hand. "Your job will be waiting for you when you're able to come back to work."

It had been a long and frustrating process, the gradual return of speech and movement. But in time Father had recovered well enough to return to the foundry, and eventually he was back to normal.

This time it was different. He was unconscious, and the doctor was not optimistic. I stayed by his side in the hospital, holding his hand and speaking to him softly.

"Do you remember when I was about eight years old and you took me to your factory?" I asked.

The day had been bright and sunny, but inside the foundry where the printing presses were manufactured, it was a different world—hot, dusty, and smoky. The noise was deafening. Clutching Father's hand, I had climbed metal stairs to an iron balcony where we looked down on a terrifying scene. A gigantic ladle suspended from an overhead track was guided into place and tipped, pouring a fiery cascade of red-hot liquid metal into molds. There was a blast of intense heat. Sparks flew and danced.

"I'll never forget that, Father," I whispered, recalling the heart-pounding sense of danger I'd felt then, and the trust I'd always had in him. I knew he'd keep me safe. Now I squeezed his hand, willing him to squeeze back, but there was no response.

◆ ◆

Ruth rushed home from Boston and spelled me at Father's bedside. I didn't want to leave, but she and Mother insisted. Not long after I reached home and climbed into my childhood bed, Father died. I was heartbroken not to have been with him.

Mother was completely shaken—we all were—but she steeled herself and got in touch with Father's relatives. Father's brother, Lazarus, called Lazar—an engineer, like Father—and Uncle Lazar's wife, Naomi, came at once. So did Grandmother White and my two cousins, Felicia and David. I had met them a few times, but I scarcely knew them. It was obvious that Mother disliked her mother-in-law and sister-in-law, and she had only grudging respect for Uncle Lazar. She was barely civil to them. I had no idea why, and when I asked her, she brushed me off. "I have my reasons."

At the funeral on a blustery January day, a handful of men from the foundry appeared in black suits. They stood beside the open grave, bare-headed and holding their fedoras, and assured Mother that Joseph White would never be forgotten, that a plaque in his memory would be mounted outside the main office.

A tall, thin man with a goatee began to read from a notebook, droning on and on about what a fine person Joseph White had been. I'd never seen him before. How did he know anything about my father? I glanced at Ruth questioningly. "Ethical Culture Society," she whispered. "Kind of a non-church. Mother's idea."

Roger leaned against Mother, crying quietly. Mother looked as though every drop of blood had been drained from her. Uncle Lazar, Aunt Naomi, and Grandmother White clung to each other as a shovelful of dirt was flung onto the plain wooden coffin. My cousins stared dolefully at the grave. Standing by the graveside, I felt only an awful numbness, as though a hole had been hollowed out inside me. Mother handed each of us a white rose she'd bought from a florist, and I stepped forward and dropped mine onto the dirt. I wondered when I'd be able to feel again, or if I ever would.

It was over. The men from R. Hoe & Company replaced their fedoras and left. The rest of us drove back to our house, and Mother served lunch, ladling out steaming bowls of pea soup. Uncle Lazar and Aunt Naomi shook their heads, saying they weren't hungry, and Grandmother White also refused the bowl Mother offered her. "I don't eat ham, Minnie," she said. "You made this soup with a ham bone."

"That's right," Mother said, her chin lifted defiantly. "I did."

"You should have known I wouldn't eat it." Grandmother

White and Mother glared at each other.

The others looked away, except for Ruth, who shook her head. I wondered what she was thinking.

The relatives did not stay long. Uncle Lazar hugged Roger and Ruth and me. "I'll do what I can to help you with your schooling, if you need it," he promised.

We thanked him, although I had no idea if we needed it or not. A few days later, I found out how much we did.

Ruth offered to go through Father's things with Mother, who sat at the dining room table, poring over a pile of bills. "Twenty-five years," she muttered. "Twenty-five years of marriage, and I never had the slightest idea of any of this."

The door to Roger's room was closed. I tapped on it and pushed it open. Roger lay on his bed, staring at the ceiling. "Go away," he growled, trying to sound older than a boy of eleven. I ruffled his hair, but he pushed my hand away.

I left Roger alone and wandered from room to room, gazing at Father's photographs that crowded every wall. The one he'd done of Mother in her shawl, lit with a flashlight, her head turned a little, her smile tentative. Another of Ruth and Roger and me at Niagara Falls, after he'd recovered from his first stroke. Pictures of flowers, birds, my butterflies, our old dog, Rover. Even though I knew there would be no more photographs, I couldn't look away. They had that much power.

On the day before Ruth had to leave for Boston and her law classes, Mother called us together at the dining room table. Ruth brewed a pot of tea and poured a glass of milk for Roger and brought him the last of the cookies sent by our neighbors.

"There's something I want to tell all of you," Mother began. "There is no way to make it any easier. The Whites are Jews. I'm talking about Lazarus, Naomi, Grandmother, and your cousins. All of them are observant Jews, meaning they obey certain laws that make not a particle of sense to me."

Roger broke off a corner of his molasses cookie and stuffed it into his mouth. I bit my knuckles. Ruth poured milk into her tea and asked calmly, "What about Father?"

"Jewish, too, of course, but not observant. He rejected all of that long before we were married, before I even met him. He told me right off about his family and asked if it mattered to me. He knew I was Catholic on one side, Baptist on the other and wanted nothing to do with either one. I said it didn't matter, but I had to be honest and tell him I've never liked Jews. In general, I mean."

Ruth and I stared at Mother, trying to take in what she was saying. "Why?" Roger piped up. He was chasing a crumb around the saucer in front of him. "Why don't you like Jews?"

"Because they're like Lazar and Naomi. They call themselves the Chosen People. They're greedy and all they care about is money. You don't see Jews taking the hard jobs. They get someone else to do their dirty work and then make a profit from it. So it's not something you want to brag about, that your own father was born and raised a Jew."

I had never heard her talk like this. And she wasn't finished.

"When the family moved from Poland to England, their name was Weis, which means "white." They changed it before they came to America, before your father was born. Grandmother White doesn't let you forget for a minute who she is. That's why she was making that fuss about not eating my soup. Jews don't eat ham. I didn't do it to deliberately insult her, but she took it that way, didn't she?"

I was speechless, but Ruth was not. "Why are you telling us this now?"

"Because someone might mention it to you, ask you questions, and I didn't want you to be surprised. I wanted you to hear it from me first."

"Is it a secret?" asked Roger.

"Not a secret, exactly. You don't talk about it, but if someone happens to ask you if you're Jewish, you should say, 'I'm not, but my father was born to a Jewish family.' And then change the subject."

"Oh," said Roger. "May I please be excused?"

Mother nodded, and Roger pushed his chair away from the table. Ruth poured herself another cup of tea.

I still hadn't said anything, mostly because I didn't know what to say, or even what to think. I didn't know any Jews. Was it true, what Mother had said about them? I'd never heard her talk this way about anybody. Did Father know how much she disliked his mother, his brother, his family? Did other people dislike them too? How did that make Father feel?

I listened to the *clink clink* of Ruth's spoon against the teacup. What Mother had just told us seemed the least important thing I'd ever learned about my father, no more important than his shoe size. What could it possibly mean to *me*?

"Uncle Lazar said he'd help us with tuition, if we need it," I said finally, because it seemed I had to say *something*.

"Well, you probably will," said Mother. "Your father was not prudent with money."

The next day Ruth got on the train for Boston, and it fell to me to visit the law offices of Calhoun and Reilly. Mr. Calhoun, a half dozen thin strands of pale hair combed in even rows across his skull, examined a single sheet of paper on his desk. He explained that, although Father had drawn up a Last Will and Testament stating that his estate was to be divided evenly in four portions among his wife and three children, there was actually no estate to speak of—just a small savings account and a house with a mortgage.

Mother was right: Father had not been prudent with money.

"You and Ruth will have enough to finish out the year," Calhoun said. "But after that, I'm afraid you're on your own."

◆◆

When I returned to college two weeks after my father's death, Madge was in our room, studying. She jumped up, exclaiming, "Oh, Peggy! I was so worried when we didn't hear from you!"

I had left her a note—"Father ill. Going home"—and I'd signed out of Brooks Hall under the housemother's suspicious eye, listing "Family emergency" under "Reason for leaving."

"My father died," I said.

I hadn't broken down in the hospital when I sat by Father's bedside, or when the doctor told us that he was dead, or later at the cemetery, or even as I lay on my bed next to Ruth's. But as I shared this news with Madge, I began to weep.

Madge threw her arms around me, gently stroking my hair as I cried. When I'd stopped sobbing and wiped my face and blown my nose, she said, "Your friend Gil called you a couple of times. He left his number."

She pointed to the slips of paper on my desk, each with the same message. But I could not bring myself to walk down the hall to the telephone and tell him about Father. I was afraid I'd start weeping again.

I was not the same Peggy White I'd been a few days earlier. My father was dead, and my mother's life was turned upside down. It had finally sunk in that I was half Jewish, whatever that meant, but I had no intention of telling anyone. And I understood that I might not be able to afford to return to classes at Columbia in the fall, if Uncle Lazar could not offer any more help.

I had missed a few classes at the start of the new semester, and the next day I stopped by to speak to my professors, explain what had happened, and find out what I needed to make up. The days passed, a monotonous routine of getting up, attending class, eating meals or skipping them—it seemed to make no difference—going to bed and then getting up again, still exhausted. I felt nothing, unless numbness could be called a feeling.

I'd been back at college for a week, and it was my turn to answer the telephone. My shift was almost over when Gil phoned.

"Peggy!" he cried. "I've been trying to reach you!"

"I know. I got your messages," I said. A lump was forming in my throat, and I struggled to speak. Finally I got the words out: "My father died." And I began to sob—again.

He murmured, "Peggy, I'm terribly sorry," and then added, "If it's all right, I'll come to see you tomorrow as soon as I finish work."

He took me to the Cafe Prague, a coffee shop owned by a Czech lady. Sitting across from me in the cracked leather booth, Gil studied me with kind, thoughtful eyes. "Tell me what happened," he said, and I recounted the story of Father's sudden death. He listened quietly, asking a question now and then. Gil reached over and squeezed my hand. I hoped he'd keep holding it, but he didn't.

Gil said he was thinking of going out west the following summer. I told him I planned to look for a summer job, but didn't mention I was worried about having enough money to continue college, because my father hadn't been "prudent with money."

We walked across the campus under a black sky full of glittering stars. Neither of us spoke. I was thinking of what might come next: a kiss, maybe? As we approached the entrance to Brooks Hall, I tried to ignore the couples embracing in shadowy corners of the portico. Gil escorted me into the reception room, where several couples sat quietly, holding hands. Should I ask him to sit down?

Gil stepped back, clutching his hat brim in both hands. "Please accept my condolences for the death of your father. I'm happy that we could see each other and talk, Peggy," he said. "May I call you again soon?"

"Of course, Gil," I said, a little surprised by his formal tone and trying to match it. "And thank you for the coffee and pastry. I enjoyed the evening."

Gil strode briskly down the walkway as the campus clock bonged eight times. I watched him go and climbed slowly to my room on the fourth floor, feeling more alone than I had ever felt in my life.

7

A Course in Photography—1922

I'D NEVER HAD MUCH INTEREST IN TAKING PICTURES. That was something Father did, and I'd been happy to help. But when I heard about a two-hour-a-week class in photography being offered, I thought of Father, borrowed a camera, and signed up.

The teacher, Clarence H. White, believed that photography was an art form, not just a simple matter of clicking the shutter to capture an image. "Experiment! Develop your capacity to see!" Mr. White urged.

I wanted to make lovely, soft-focus pictures like his, each one carefully planned. That kind of planning, I realized now, was what my father did. I could almost hear his voice explaining why this angle was better than that one, why the lighting must be adjusted just so.

One weekend on a visit home, I asked Mother what had happened to Father's old camera. "I don't know what's become of it," she said. "He stopped taking pictures a year or so ago, and the camera disappeared. He might have given it away, or sold it. But it's gone."

Gone? I could hardly believe it—another link to my father, lost. But a week later Mother telephoned. "I have a surprise for you," she said. "It will be here the next time you come home."

She had bought me a camera. Her budget was tight, she had Roger to feed and clothe, but somehow she'd managed to find twenty dollars for a second-hand Ica Reflex. It was rare for her to buy me something that she would not have considered necessary or practical.

I was stunned. I tried to thank her, to tell her how much it meant to me, but she brushed me off. "It has a cracked lens," she said. "That will make it more of a challenge."

I proudly carried the German-made camera into class. It was the old-fashioned kind, like Father's and Mr. White's, that used glass plates, rather than film. The crack wouldn't matter, because I wanted to make artistic photographs like those Clarence White was famous for. It became my favorite class. Two hours a week didn't seem like nearly enough to learn everything I wanted to know.

I was sure I wanted to be a herpetologist. That had not changed. I still kept pet snakes caged in my dormitory room, still dreamed of going on exciting expeditions. But I suspected that the scientists on those expeditions were always men. How could I ever make a name for myself in a man's world? I remembered what Miss Fowler, the phrenologist, had told me: "Take photographs of the places you visit and the sights you see." Those scientific men would surely need a photographer on their exotic trips, and I could be that photographer!

I now had a goal and a path to reach it.

◆◆

Every week or two Gil telephoned. We fell into a predictable routine, going to a movie or a free concert and ending the evening at the Cafe Prague. The waitress brought two cups of coffee and a plate of *palačinky*, those delicious Czech pancakes, without being asked. We talked about the work Gil was doing and about my photography class, but I didn't mention that I now saw photography as my way into a life of scientific adventure. I wasn't sure he'd understand that.

Sometimes he held my hand, but still he didn't kiss me—just walked me to my dormitory, said good night, and left. I wondered if there was another girl he was in love with. Or maybe he had once been in love with a girl who broke his heart. I didn't ask, because we didn't talk about such things. He reminded me of Father in so many ways. Maybe that's why I was attracted to him. Even his silences felt familiar.

◆◆

The semester was almost over and I was in a panic. I needed a job. Madge suggested I apply to be a counselor at a summer camp in Connecticut. Her parents had sent her to Camp Agaming every year when she was young, and the previous summer she'd worked there as a counselor. Now she was going back, and she promised to ask her lawyer father to write a recommendation for me on his firm's letterhead.

After only a few months of Mr. White's classes, I worked up the courage to apply for the position of photography instructor, and I was hired! I would also be a nature counselor, taking campers on walks to introduce them to snakes and butterflies and teach them to identify plants. It seemed like the perfect combination of my two great interests: photography and natural science. I knew just enough about each to convince myself that I could keep the young campers' attention.

I had finished my last final exam—I felt sure I'd done well in all of them—and was packing up when Gil telephoned and suggested that we meet at the Cafe Prague. I slid into our usual booth and launched into an enthusiastic description of my summer job.

"While you're cooped up in your lab," I told Gil, "I'll be out in the fresh air and sunshine, teaching the campers to take pictures and showing them the wonders of the outdoors. I'll bet I learn as much as the little girls do!"

"Sounds swell," Gil said, sipping his coffee.

Sounds swell? That was all he had to say? Not a word about what an ideal opportunity this was for me—that I'd be combining my old love for the natural world with my new love for photography, and being paid for it? I'd hoped for more from him.

I tried again to spark some enthusiasm. "Camp Agaming isn't too far from Bound Brook. Maybe you could come up some weekend."

But Gil looked away. "I won't be at Calco after this week. I've accepted a position as assistant professor in pharmacy at Oregon Agricultural College in Corvallis. That's where I got my bachelor's degree."

"Oh," I said. I shouldn't have been surprised. He'd mentioned before that he'd been thinking of going out west, but I wasn't expecting it so soon. "Well, congratulations!" I said as heartily as I could manage.

Gil walked me back to my residence hall, and we stopped under the portico. "Good-bye, Peg. I've enjoyed our friendship." He held out his hand, and I shook it.

"Thank you. I've enjoyed it, too."

I climbed the three flights of stairs to my room and sat hunched on the edge of my bed, trying to sort through my feelings. I didn't think I was in love with Gil. How would I even know if I was? He was the first boy—man—I'd ever gone out with. But I was awfully disappointed—not only was he not in love with me and hadn't kissed me, but he hadn't shown any interest in what so deeply interested *me*.

Madge burst in and suddenly stopped. She peered at me.

"You all right, Peg? You look kind of down. Something happen with Gil?"

"No, of course not," I said, mustering a false smile. "Nothing at all."

◆◆

"Who would like to hear a different story of Sleeping Beauty?" I asked a group of talkative ten-year-olds on their first evening at Camp Agaming. We sat on logs arranged around a crackling campfire somewhere in the hills of western Connecticut.

I produced a chrysalis—the "sleeping beauty"—that I was carrying in my pocket. In a second, the girls had stopped chattering and were clustered around me.

"Once upon a time," I began, "this little chrysalis became the home of a very ugly caterpillar." I let them pass it around. They were full of questions. Was it still in there? What was it doing? I explained how the caterpillar was indeed in the chrysalis, silently changing from something ugly into something beautiful. "Soon it will emerge as a butterfly, and if we're lucky, we might see it happen."

"Is it magic, Miss Peggy?" asked a little girl with solemn blue eyes.

"All of nature has a little bit of magic," I said.

Some campers stayed for two weeks, but others had been packed off by their families for a month or longer, and I was constantly challenged to find ways to engage them. When we went out on a photographing expedition early each morning, I tried to teach them how to see, the way Clarence White had taught me. "Slow down!" I instructed them. "Look carefully."

Mr. White composed each photograph with infinite care before he finally committed to clicking the shutter. He insisted that a photographer left nothing to chance. "Chance is a poor photographer," he said. "Think like an artist. Study your subject."

This advice was lost on the girls. They wanted to rush off with their Kodak Brownie box cameras and take pictures of everything in sight.

After the campers were worn out from riding horses and swimming in the chilly waters of Bantam Lake and were sound asleep, Madge and I rushed to the makeshift darkroom to develop their rolls of film and print their snapshots, ready to show the campers their pictures the next morning.

On my free days I hiked alone to the highest point I could find. A fence spoiled the view, but I'd been fearlessly balancing on fence rails and crossing streams on narrow logs since I was the age of my campers, and I climbed over. Crawling as close to the cliff edge as possible, I lay flat on the ground, my camera balanced on a rock, the whole valley spread out below me. Sometimes I had to make several attempts to get the perfect shot, because it started to rain, or clouds interfered, or the angle of the sun wasn't quite right.

I observed my eighteenth birthday by packing a lunch and hitching a ride to Mohawk Mountain, some twenty miles from the camp. Most girls would have wanted to celebrate with a party, but I was more interested in taking at least one breathtaking picture.

I was paid a small salary, but tuition would soon come due for my sophomore year—nearly seven hundred dollars—and I wasn't sure how much Uncle Lazar was willing to contribute. Perhaps I could make some money from the pictures I was taking. Campers were required to send a postcard home each week. If I took pictures of each girl in front of her cabin, lounging on her bunk, practicing archery, or paddling a canoe, and made them into postcards, the girls would have something personal to mail home. Their families surely would clamor for more cards to send to Grandma and aunts and uncles.

I charged a nickel apiece, and orders poured in by the dozen.

Encouraged, I expanded my original idea and took a number of photographs of the camp: the carved wooden sign at the end of the road, a row of canoes drawn up on the shore, the archery range framed through a drawn bow. I went into Litchfield and photographed the pretty white church on the green and the old foundry with its bronze cannons. I had a hunch summer visitors would like scenes of this quaint colonial village. I took a few sample postcards to a gift shop on the main street and returned to camp with an order for five hundred postcards. I couldn't believe my good luck, but now I had to figure out a way to pay for the chemicals to print my photographs before I could collect a cent.

"Oh, don't worry about it," Madge said airily. "I'll be glad to help you, and you don't need to pay me." Madge never had to worry about money the way I did.

The cards were a hit, and campers and their families continued to clamor for them. I knew I was on to something. Madge and I worked frantically to keep up with our duties as counselors and stayed up night after night to keep up with the orders that poured in.

I sold nearly two thousand cards. Even after paying for supplies, I made a small profit. I now saw that it was possible to earn money doing something I loved.

◆◆

Even with the postcard money and my salary from Camp Agaming and the help Uncle Lazar had offered, I still didn't have nearly enough to pay my tuition. Mother and I sat at our dining room table, staring hopelessly at the figures she'd laid out on a sheet of lined paper. Mother had taken a job selling insurance policies, but she had only limited success. She decided to get rid of our car, since she had no desire to learn to drive, but that money went to repair the furnace and pay off bills.

I felt sick. It seemed as though I would have to drop out after just one year. Give up herpetology, give up photography, give up everything I loved. My father was dead. Gil was gone. I had no money, no future, nothing to look forward to. I'd never felt worse, and there was absolutely nothing I could do except to start looking for a job.

8

The Mungers—1922

MOTHER HELPED ME PREPARE A LIST OF PLACES WHERE I might apply for a position. The insurance company where she worked, though not very successfully, could possibly use help in the office, answering the phone, filing, and so on. A department store in Plainfield had been advertising for help, and there were small shops in Bound Brook that might hire. "Maybe the pet shop," she said, and for a minute I brightened.

But nothing came of any of these ideas. Classes at Columbia would start soon, but I couldn't allow myself to think about that. Instead, I tried to make a list of the things I could do. *Photography*, I wrote. *Working with children.*

"Sewing," Mother said. "You sew very nicely."

Seamstress, I added.

Roger came home from the Mungers' where he'd been mowing the grass. "Mr. Henry asked me to tell you to come over. He and Miss Jessie want to talk to you."

"Did he say what they want to talk about?"

Roger shrugged. "No. I told them you were home, and they asked about school, and I said you weren't going back, and they said to give you the message."

I had visited our neighbors before I'd left for Camp Agaming, when I'd taken them a jar of Mother's strawberry jam. They greeted me warmly now and ushered me into the parlor where I'd spent so many hours reading to Miss Jessie. Mr. Henry brought in a pot of peppermint tea and a plate of cookies.

"So, Margaret," Mr. Henry began when we were settled. "You've finished your first year of college. I hear that you did very well in your courses."

"Yes, I did," I replied. "But how did you know that?"

"Roger told us. He comes by to help us out from time to time," said Miss Jessie. "Also, Henry knows quite a few people on the faculty at Columbia, and he inquired about you. They supported Roger's view of your accomplishments."

I don't know which surprised me more—that Roger had spoken about me to the Mungers, or that Mr. Henry had spoken about me to my professors. I had no idea he even knew who they were.

"And are you still intending to continue with your study of herpetology?" asked Mr. Henry.

"Yes, I am, but not until later. I plan to find a job and work for a year or two and then return to school." I had no intention of telling them about my financial troubles.

The Mungers exchanged glances. "Well, my dear Margaret," began Mr. Henry, "Miss Jessie and I are happy to tell you that we've decided to pay your college tuition and expenses for the coming year."

"Longer, if things go well," added Miss Jessie.

"And we anticipate that they will," said Mr. Henry.

Speechless, I stared at them, hardly daring to believe what I'd heard. Could it be true? They were offering to pay for a year of college? This could change my entire life!

66

"Thank you for having so much faith in me," I stammered when I finally managed to find my voice. "I promise you won't regret loaning me the money, and I promise I'll repay it, starting the day I graduate."

"Oh, no, my dear!" Miss Jessie trilled. "We'll hear no talk of a loan. What we do ask, though, is that when you have achieved success, you will seek out another young person in financial need and help her."

"Or him," said Mr. Henry. "We're investing in you and your future, my dear."

"And another deserving student," added Miss Jessie.

The Mungers laid out their plans for me. They believed the University of Michigan would be a better place for me to study herpetology with Professor Alexander Ruthven, whose reputation they knew.

Not return to New York? Go to Ann Arbor instead? My mind was in such a confused state that I had to ask them to repeat what they had just told me.

"Now about this postcard business of yours," said Miss Munger. *How on earth did she know about that?* I wondered. "Roger, again, was our informant—he's quite proud of both of his sisters, you know. It's clever and industrious of you, Margaret, but you can find better ways to invest your time and energy, and it's sure to be hard on your eyes, spending all that time in the darkroom. Also, you should have an enjoyable social life, but you must dress the part. Buy some nice clothes, the proper kind for a young student. We know you won't be extravagant. It's not in your nature. That much is clear."

"Silk stockings," I murmured. Could this really be happening? These kind people, making such a generous offer?

"Yes, my dear, silk stockings! And a few smart dresses and— for goodness sake—a coat that fits you properly."

"Of course, Miss Munger." I hadn't realized she ever noticed what I wore.

"You would look terribly attractive in a rose-colored dress," Miss Jessie mused thoughtfully. "Please leave the brown and gray ones in Bound Brook."

"Now go home and start packing," Mr. Henry instructed. "A bank account is being established for you in Ann Arbor. We know you'll use it wisely. It will be replenished when necessary. We've also taken the liberty of buying you a train ticket. You are to leave within a fortnight. I've sent a letter to Dr. Ruthven, recommending you. Look him up as soon as you get there and sign up for his courses."

I hugged my benefactors—I'd never done that before—and thanked them over and over, not knowing how to express my gratitude adequately. Then I rushed home to tell Mother the news. She was as amazed as I was at the Mungers' offer. "Are you sure?" she asked. I said I was sure I understood it all, but I was as shocked as she was. "It's a loan, of course," Mother said firmly. "I hope you assured them that we'll pay back every penny."

"That's exactly what I told them," I said, and repeated what the Mungers had said about helping another needy student in the future. "Miss Jessie also said I should buy some new clothes, and that I should not skimp but get whatever I need."

Mother harrumphed. "Then you must keep track of whatever you spend on clothes, although I frankly can't see that it's at all necessary," she said. "What you already have is perfectly serviceable. One or two new dresses, perhaps, but certainly no more. It's that much less you will owe the Mungers."

That night I wrote to Madge, explaining that I would not be returning to school and describing the exciting news. "I'm just sorry that we won't be roommates."

I thought of Tubby and Sara Jane and wondered how they

were getting along. I'd tried to reach them, to tell them how Miss Fowler's reading of my head was actually starting to work out. But they had both worked as waitresses in Ocean City all summer and then gone away with their parents for family vacations, and there was never time to get together before they left for college.

Two weeks later I boarded a train bound for Michigan, my money problems miraculously solved, and my future emerging as mysteriously as a photographic negative in the developing bath.

Michigan—1922

I'D BEEN ASSIGNED A ROOM IN BETSY BARBOUR HOUSE.
My single room on the third floor of "Betsy's" was cramped and
dark, but the two parlors downstairs were bright and elegant, one
with a grand piano and a fireplace, the other with windows looking out on the lush green lawn.

There were far more men than women at the university, and
the telephone on the third floor hall rang constantly for other
girls. It was clear from the first that I would not fit in here any
better than I had at Barnard. Most of the girls on my floor were
not particularly friendly. They thought I was odd, peculiar even,
for keeping snakes in glass terrariums next to my bed. In my first
week at Betsy's, Oscar, a handsomely banded milk snake, escaped
and slithered down the hall, terrifying an unsuspecting girl who
assumed he must be poisonous. I explained that Oscar was quite
benign. "Red on yellow, deadly fellow, red on black, venom lack,"
I told her helpfully, but she screamed, "I don't care! I don't *care*!
Get that thing away from me! Why do you even have it here?"

"But why should I not have snakes? I'm going to be a
herpetologist!"

It was not a good beginning. I heard one girl refer to me as "the snake charmer in 307," and I didn't think it was meant as a compliment.

Florence was an exception. She liked to come around to watch when I was feeding the snakes, dropping mice into their cages. "You're not odd," she said, "but you are definitely eccentric."

No one had ever told me I was eccentric. "Is that good or bad?" I asked.

She shrugged, watching Oscar go for the mouse. "Depends. But you certainly get noticed."

I had been in Ann Arbor for about a month when Florence suggested we go to a dance at a nearby church. I dreaded another dance like those in high school, but I said yes.

I had used the Mungers' money to buy a dress of knit crepe in the soft rose color Miss Jessie had recommended, the most expensive dress I'd ever owned, and I wore it to the dance. It must have caught the eye of every male in the dingy basement. I danced every dance.

"See? I told you you'd get noticed," Florence said enviously as we were walking back to Betsy's. After that, she still came to my room to look at the snakes, but she never again suggested going to the church dances.

So I went alone. I met more boys and danced a lot, but I soon learned not to talk about my plan to travel to exotic places and take pictures. "You can't be serious, Peggy," one boy said, laughing, and another told me, "That's not what girls do." If I wanted to be popular, it was better to talk about *their* dreams, not mine. I did, and it worked. I was invited to lots of parties, as long as I didn't let any boy know who I really was.

I had enrolled in the zoology department and registered for two of Professor Ruthven's classes in herpetology—most of his research was on garter snakes. I studied hard and generally pulled good grades in all my classes, and I might have had straight A's if

71

I had not become so caught up with photography. I roamed the campus and the town with my camera, always alert for the next possible shot. I loved the old buildings with their steeply pitched gables and arched windows, and I was fascinated by trains, from the enormous locomotives to the abstract patterns of their small mechanical parts. I'd always had a variety of interests, but this was different. Suddenly I had a passion, and it was all-consuming.

Frank Howarth, a new acquaintance who was studying business administration and cultivating a thin mustache, invited me to go for a walk on a golden autumn Sunday afternoon and asked where I'd like to go.

"To the railroad station."

Frank raised an eyebrow, but he agreed.

He stood by patiently while I focused on a locomotive taking on coal and water. I moved in close and set up my shot. "Isn't this exciting, Frank?" I shouted over the racket of the steam-bellowing monster. I couldn't hear his reply.

"You're certainly not like other girls," Frank said after an hour or two of being ignored while I took pictures. "Shall we stop for a bite to eat?"

He chose a tearoom near the campus. Ravenous after an afternoon of photographing pistons and wheels, I gobbled up a plate of dainty sandwiches. Frank mostly watched. "I'm the business manager for *The Michiganensian*," he said. "The student yearbook. You should come by and meet the editor. I think he'd be interested in some of the photographs you took this afternoon."

A few days later I found the office of the *'Ensian* and introduced myself to the editor, Harold Martin. "I'm Peggy White, and I'm a photographer."

"Is that so?" Martin drawled and smiled mockingly. "Bring in some samples of your work. I can use some good pictures of campus buildings, if you have any."

I took it as a challenge. Two weeks later I was back in Martin's office with a portfolio of prints. He spread them out on a table and studied each one. The mocking smile was gone. "I don't think I've seen anything quite like these before. They're like paintings. Somehow you've captured the personality in each building."

"I've studied with Clarence White," I explained.

He glanced up at the mention of White's name. "He taught you well. As of now, you're a staff photographer."

From then on I was out taking pictures whenever I could spare time from my studies and my busy social life. I'd always wanted to be popular, and now, suddenly, I was. I seemed to be making up for lost time.

One of my admirers was Joe Vlack, also a photographer for the 'Ensian. Joe was twenty-two, tall and thin with unruly hair, rumpled clothes, and a long, narrow face that made him look older. "I have an idea for some pictures," he'd say, and we would go off on another photographic adventure.

Joe suggested photographing the clock tower in the Engineering Shops Building. "The best view is from the men's toilet on the fourth floor," Joe said. "You can get a great angle from there, but I don't know if—"

"I'm game," I said.

We waited until classes were over and climbed to the fourth floor. Joe made sure the coast was clear, and we shut ourselves into the toilet and latched the door. I balanced on the seat and rested my camera on the window ledge above it. I was setting up the shot when someone knocked. Joe called out, "Sorry—occupied! Come back later!"

The building grew quiet. I worked until Joe remembered that the janitor always locked up the building as soon as the clock struck six. "Just one more shot," I said, and then I grabbed my camera and we fled.

Some of Joe's ideas were frightening. "There's a magnificent view from the roof of Engineering Shops," he said. "I know how to get us out there, if you're not afraid."

"Afraid?" I responded scornfully. "Let's do it."

"Wear trousers and shoes with rubber soles. Gloves would be a good idea. Fasten your camera to your belt. You'll need to have both hands free."

The next evening, dressed like a mountaineer, I signed out of the dormitory "to study in the library" and returned to the engineering building. Joe had persuaded the janitor to leave a side door unlocked and was waiting for me. He had already climbed out through a classroom window on the fourth floor, fastened one end of a rope to a cleat, tossed the rest of the rope over the ridgeline, and anchored the other end on the opposite side. I was supposed to use the rope to haul myself up the steep slope of the roof. My stomach lurched and my hands started to sweat.

"I'll be right behind you," he promised, "in case you start to slide back."

I was glad I'd worked on strength in my arms in gym class. If I was going to be part of scientific expeditions and take photographs in difficult places, I needed to be physically strong.

My throat tight with fear, I scrambled up the side of the roof, planting one foot ahead of the other and hanging onto the rope. Joe was right; the view of the campus was magnificent. I got the pictures I wanted, sure that no one had ever done anything like this before—the knowledge of that was intoxicating.

A few nights later, sitting across from me at the Royal Cafe, Joe stirred a third spoonful of sugar into his coffee and laid out another idea: descending into the tunnels that ran beneath the streets of Ann Arbor.

"Let's go," I said, and we left as soon as he'd gulped the rest of his coffee.

He lifted off a heavy manhole cover and plunged into the

darkness, calling up to me, "Hand me your camera, Peg. And watch your step on the ladder. It's pretty slippery."

I crawled down one rung at a time, clinging to the rung above me. It was dank and fetid and I was not eager to stay long, but I was able to photograph some valves and pipes. When we saw the prints, Joe pronounced the photographs first rate.

Whenever some new machine was assembled in his class in the Engineering Shops, Joe called me. "You'll love this thing," he'd say, and I'd race over and we'd study it together. Joe had a knack for thinking of the most interesting angles for me to photograph.

Still, I fretted that my photographs weren't turning out as well as I wanted. I had Clarence White's pictures as the standard I aimed for, and I tried to use his methods, like stretching one of my precious silk stockings over the lens to soften the edges of the image. But the composition was not elegant enough, my use of natural light never achieved the subtle effect I wanted. I knew I had a long way to go to become as accomplished as Mr. White.

Joe disagreed. "Don't be so hard on yourself, Peggy. Your pictures are really works of art. You're going to be famous—I'm positive of that. In fact, I've never been surer of anything in my life."

Sometimes I was too tired to meet him, but he refused to take no for an answer. "This is for your *future*, Peg," he'd argue. And I'd give in on the chance that the new piece of machinery he insisted I photograph was worth the exhaustion the next day.

Joe Vlack was the only one I knew who believed in me as much as I believed in myself. Maybe even more.

Toward the end of the semester, Dr. Ruthven called me to his office. I was nervous about this interview. Maybe he'd heard about my picture-taking and thought I wasn't concentrating enough on my coursework.

The professor's desk was piled high with stacks of papers, publications, and reference books. Framed certificates and award

*Clarence White's dreamy photographs
influenced Margaret's early work.*

plaques hung haphazardly on the wall. It had been snowing heavily, and his galoshes sat in a spreading puddle of water. Dr. Ruthven leaned back in a swivel chair, lit a pipe, and puffed on it. The scent of cherry-flavored tobacco filled the crowded office. I perched on the edge of my seat, nervously tucking my fingers beneath my thighs to keep my hands from shaking.

"Miss White, you are enrolled as a student of zoology, and you're doing well in my classes. Now I'd like you to tell me, if you will, what your plans might be for the future."

"I'm studying to be a herpetologist," I replied, knowing that's what I was expected to say.

"And may I ask what has led you to that particular field of study?"

I explained that ever since childhood I'd had an interest in living creatures of all kinds. I described my collection of caterpillars and my observations of the moment a butterfly emerged. I told him about encountering the hognose snake with my father, marveling at the snake's behavior, and bringing the snake home. I talked about Oscar and the other snakes I kept in my room.

The professor listened, prodding me along occasionally, gesturing with the stem of his pipe. "I understand that you have other interests as well. I've heard many favorable comments about your photographs."

Maybe this was the time to speak honestly about my passion for photography. So I described my classes with Clarence White, but I omitted any mention of my escapades with Joe Vlack, which probably violated all sorts of university policies.

Dr. Ruthven knocked the ash from his pipe and refilled it, tamped the tobacco, struck a match, and puffed while I anxiously waited. "Tell me what you wish to accomplish in the world," he said.

I hesitated, thinking of the best way to answer. I loved my "herps," but I no longer saw them as my main focus. I enjoyed writing, and I knew I was good at it—my papers were always graded A-plus—but I believed my life was heading in a new and challenging direction.

Looking the distinguished scientist boldly in the eye, I admitted, "I want to become a photographer."

He blew a perfect smoke ring. "I assume you mean that you wish to concentrate on scientific subjects," he said. "And not, I trust, to snap pictures of babies for their parents to display on the mantelpiece." His tone made it clear that was not an acceptable choice.

"I like to take pictures and I like to write, too. I hope to become a news photographer and reporter." Then I added, "I intend to work hard to be a very good one."

"Well put, Miss White!" Dr. Ruthven exclaimed. "Now let me think about how I may be able to help you along in this interesting trajectory you envision. We'll talk again."

I sailed out of Dr. Ruthven's smoky office and headed straight for the 'Ensian, in search of Joe Vlack. Joe grinned when I told him about my conversation with the professor. "You're on your way, Peg. There'll be no stopping you."

Successes—1922

THE *'ENSIAN* ACCEPTED A DOZEN OF MY PHOTOGRAPHS. Harold Martin was particularly struck by a nighttime picture of a building, lights glowing in every window. "I'm not sure how you did that," the editor said admiringly. There were photographs of a building's harsh lines muffled in snow, a classical column shown in its geometric simplicity, the dome of the observatory cloaked in shadow. Harold wanted them all. Each would be published as a full page, in a special section.

Suddenly everything seemed to be going my way, but I still had not been kissed. Philip Cole, the president of the photography club, was alone with me in the darkroom, working on prints for the *'Ensian*, and I'd just taken a set of prints from the fixative when Philip clasped my wrist. "Peg," he said, "you're the most interesting, the most beautiful, the most desirable girl I've ever met." He hesitated and then stammered, "And I want very much to kiss you."

He bent closer. It was about to happen! But I hesitated. I liked Philip, but I wasn't *crazy* about him. And I wanted to be crazy about the first boy who kissed me. Otherwise, it wouldn't mean anything. That was *my* theory.

"No, Philip," I said, "I think that would be a mistake. I'm afraid it would spoil our professional relationship."

He sighed. "I don't agree, but I do understand." We went back to making prints.

There were others. Before everyone left for the Christmas holidays, Fritz Snyder, a senior and the president of the men's glee club, invited me to a party at the Sigma Chi fraternity house. I wore another of my new dresses, this one "Parrish blue," for Maxfield Parrish, an artist noted for his brilliant colors. I had also taken the bold step of cutting my hair and wore it in a smooth bob. I felt extremely stylish, and I knew I was making a much better impression than I had with snakes wrapped around my arms.

At the height of the party Fritz rounded up three of his fraternity brothers and announced, "This is dedicated to our own sweetheart, Peg White." The quartet serenaded me with their famous song, "The Sweetheart of Sigma Chi." I was the center of attention, and I loved it.

Joe Vlack was one of my favorite escorts. He kept his rivals at bay by proposing intriguing photographic projects, but to me he was just a good pal, sure to be there when I needed him, always cheering me on.

◆ ◆

A few days after the Sigma Chi party I made the long trip home for the holidays. Mother was disturbed by the changes she saw in me, beginning with my shockingly bobbed hair. "I'm afraid you're becoming superficial, Margaret," she said sternly.

Ruth was still wearing drab and dreary dresses like those we'd worn in high school, the same thick cotton stockings and clumsy shoes. She looked like an old maid, and I wondered if she would end up as one. She seemed sad—had she always? I loved Ruth, but I felt I had less in common with my sister than I did with the girls who lived on my hall. Roger had grown an inch or two since last summer, and somehow I felt more comfortable with my little brother than I did with Mother or Ruth.

Sara Jane Cassidy and Tubby Luf were both home from college. We'd hardly seen each other since the summer after our high school graduation, and except for exchanging a few letters when we first left, we'd somehow lost touch. But, eager to demonstrate our new sophistication as college girls, we made a date for lunch at the Queen City Hotel, the most elegant eating place in Plainfield.

Mother thought this was pure foolishness. "Why don't you just invite your friends to come here? I could fix some hot soup, and I have a jar of the sour cherries I put up last summer that would make a nice pie."

I made excuses. "The girls have their hearts set on the Queen City."

Tubby had learned to drive and would pick us up in her father's Model T Ford. More foolishness, Mother declared; we could easily have taken the streetcar to Plainfield. It was the last straw, then, when I appeared wearing a smartly tailored burgundy dress with a matching jacket, another outfit financed by the Mungers. "Silk stockings!" Mother exclaimed when she saw me. "In this weather? Have you lost all your common sense?"

Tubby and Sara Jane pulled up, honking the horn. All three of us were dressed to the nines in our best flapper dresses with skirts up to the knees, and Sara Jane even sported a raccoon coat. Tubby was studying at the women's college at Rutgers, and Sara Jane was at Bucknell out in Pennsylvania. She could hardly wait to tell us she was considering getting pinned to a fraternity boy she'd met in the drama club.

We ordered expensive oysters and roast beef, and Sara Jane regaled us with the virtues of her new flame. "He plays the leading man in most of the Cap and Dagger productions," she said. "If I wear his pin, then it's like being engaged to be engaged."

"He sounds wonderful," I said, "but do you really want to settle down with just one boy at this point? Isn't it more fun to go out with lots of boys?"

My friends looked at me quizzically. "Is that what you're doing, Peg? Going out with lots of boys?"

"Well, yes," I admitted. "They all want to take me out, and I hardly ever say no, at least not the first time."

"Aren't you afraid you'll get a reputation?" Tubby asked with a worried look.

"For what? Being a good dancer? No, I'm not worried—I'm eighteen, and I haven't even been kissed yet!"

The girls gaped at me. "I think you're setting some kind of a record, Peg," Sara Jane said.

"I'll drink to that," Tubby said, raising her water glass. Laughing, she proposed a toast to my unkissed state coming to an end in the new year, to Sara Jane getting pinned to the fraternity boy, and to her own fond hope that the interesting boy who sat next to her in Medieval Literature would notice her and ask her out.

We, who had always been such studious linsey-woolsies, hardly mentioned our college classes, although I did tell them about my fascination with photography. Mother would have frowned and told us how disappointed she was that three of the smartest girls in our graduating class had all become superficial. But for that one afternoon together, we didn't care.

◆◆

Ruth and I were in the bedroom we had shared as children, lying in our separate beds. "Ruth?" I whispered into the darkness. "Are you still awake?"

"Yes."

"Ruth, have you ever been kissed?" When she didn't answer, I hurried on, "You don't have to answer that. It's none of my business. But I haven't, not yet, and I'm wondering if you could give me some sisterly advice—how I ought to feel about a boy before I let him kiss me."

Silence from the other bed. I wondered if I should apologize for asking such a personal question.

"Yes," Ruth replied at last, "I have been kissed, by a man I loved very much, and I didn't have to stop and wonder if it was the right thing. I didn't care if it was or if it wasn't." I heard her start to cry.

"Ruth?" I sat up, straining to see in the darkness. "Ruth, I'm sorry, I didn't mean to upset you."

"It's all right," she said. "I don't mind telling you about it. I fell in love, and he was crazy about me. He asked me to marry him, and I accepted. This was last summer—you were in Connecticut. But Mother refused to allow it."

I climbed out of my bed and crossed over to her bed. "Why haven't I heard about any of this until now?" I asked.

Ruth was blowing her nose. "Because Mother didn't want you or anyone else to know about my indiscretion. That's what she called it—an indiscretion."

"But *why*? Why the big secret?"

"Dennis's mother is Irish but his father is Chinese and he owns a laundry in Lowell, north of Boston. It was the only way he could make a living after he came to this country. Dennis works in a Chinese restaurant in Boston. That's where I met him. We got acquainted. Then we began to meet secretly."

I reached for her hand and squeezed it. "Tell me what happened," I whispered.

"Oh, Peg, I was so much in love! When he asked me to marry him, I said yes without a second's hesitation. But there is a lot of discrimination against the Chinese. I don't know why I ever thought Mother would allow it, but one day I gathered all my courage and made the trip down from Boston to tell her I wanted to bring a friend to meet her. I didn't tell her how serious I was about him. She asked his full name, and I couldn't lie. She'd know the minute she saw him. She said, 'Ruth, if you don't break this off immediately, I will disown you. I will not speak to you again.'"

"Mother said *that*? But she married a Jew!"

"She did, but she kept it a secret, didn't she? Not a word until after Father died! If she doesn't want us telling people we're half Jewish, what do you imagine she'd say if one of her daughters married a Chinaman?"

"And you did what she told you? You broke off with him?" I bristled, although frankly I was as shocked as Mother must have been.

"I knew what my life would be like if I didn't. Uncle Lazar would probably object too, and since he's helping with my tuition, I'd have to drop out of college. Everyone I know would turn their backs on me. Maybe even you, Peg!"

"I wouldn't have turned my back, Ruth. I would have wanted you to be happy."

Ruth shook her head and choked back a sob. "I had to let him go."

"Oh, dear Ruth," I sighed. "How hard it must have been for you! But someone more suitable will come along, and you'll fall in love again."

"No," Ruth said. "I've never been attractive to men. Except for Dennis, they don't look at me twice. Please don't say anything to Mother. I promised I wouldn't tell you, but I think you ought to know."

I leaned down and stroked Ruth's wet cheek, and then I crept back to my own bed and lay listening to her quiet weeping. My sister *had* been kissed, and now her heart was broken. I ached for her. How could Mother have been so cruel, just because the man was Chinese?

But something else troubled me: Chinese were disliked, and Jews were disliked, too. Would people react the way Mother did to Dennis when they found out I was Jewish? Mother and Father had kept it a secret for years, so obviously they'd been ashamed of it. Was it just as bad if you were only *half*? How hard was it going to be to keep that a secret? And would I be able to do it?

Chappie—1923

WHEN I LEFT FOR ANN ARBOR AFTER NEW YEAR'S, Roger clung to my hand, begging me to come back soon. "It's lonesome here without you," he said. "And Mother's always mad at me."

"It's not you she's mad at," I assured him. "It's because she's lonesome, too. I'll come as often as I can." I wasn't sure, though, that I could keep my word.

A few days after I returned to campus, I was on my way into the cafeteria on the West Quad for lunch. I had just stepped into the revolving door when I noticed a tall, handsome man on his way out. He noticed me, too.

"How do you do," he said, smiling, and I replied, "How do *you* do," and smiled back.

We were so busy smiling that the door kept revolving, and neither of us exited.

"Glad to meet you," said the dark-eyed stranger, who was indeed *quite* tall, at least six feet, with the shoulders of a football player, and *quite* handsome.

"Likewise," I said, and the door revolved again.

I could have made my escape then, had my usual bowl of soup, and gone on with my life. But I did not. He gave the door another firm push, and we went around still another time, both of us laughing.

"We must meet again," he said. "How about this evening?"

"I have a paper due tomorrow," I answered. "Maybe another time."

"I won't take no for an answer," he said. "This door keeps turning until you agree to meet me tonight at the Seal."

The Seal was the university seal embedded at the Diag, where two diagonal paths crossed on the quadrangle between the main buildings. It was a traditional meeting place. "Yes!" I cried. "The answer is yes!"

The door stopped turning, and we stepped out. "On official forms I'm Everett Chapman, but everyone except my mother calls me Chappie. And you've just agreed to meet me at eight tonight. Your name, please?"

"Margaret White on official forms, but everyone except my mother calls me Peg. Eight o'clock at the Seal, Peg to meet Chappie," I said and hurried away.

I finished my project in the zoology lab, and, stomach rumbling—I'd forgotten about lunch—sat through a discussion of *Paradise Lost* in an English class on the works of John Milton. Then, pelted with biting crystals of snow and blasted by a relentless arctic wind, I rushed back to my room to drop off my books before heading out again into the frigid Michigan winter.

Chappie and I reached the Seal almost at the same time. He grabbed my arm and, our heads lowered against the wind, we hurried along snowy sidewalks leading away from the campus. "I know you were expecting to go to the Royal Cafe," Chappie said, "because that's where everybody goes. But everybody knows you there and I want you all to myself."

That caught my attention. *I want you all to myself.*

At a rundown diner, Chappie picked a booth next to a steamy window. Without asking what I'd like, he ordered melted cheese sandwiches for both of us.

"My favorite," he explained.

Melted cheese happened to be mine, too, although by then I was so hungry I could have chewed the leg on the table. I ate while Chappie talked.

Everett Chapman was a senior studying electrical engineering, and he was twenty-two. He specialized in electric welding, about which I knew nothing but was now eager to learn. He had a whimsical sense of humor, but underneath the easy manner I sensed a person who worked hard and took life seriously. I may have taken my first step toward falling in love with him in that dingy diner over a melted cheese sandwich.

We made it back to the dorm before my 10:30 curfew that night, and I did not have to wait for his first kiss. It was everything I had longed for—his arms around me, his lips on mine, his breath on my cheek.

We had so much in common! If we went to a movie, we talked about it afterward and almost always agreed on whether it was a good movie or not. We saw plays put on by the drama department: *The Importance of Being Earnest* by Oscar Wilde, and *Volpone* by Ben Johnson, about a lecherous old miser who pretends to be fatally ill. We went dancing every chance we got, and I learned to dance the Charleston to songs like "Ballin' the Jack" and "The Sheik of Araby."

We read to each other. Milton:

> *The mind is its own place, and in itself*
> *Can make a heav'n of hell, a hell of heav'n.*

And Robert Frost:

> *Two roads diverged in a wood, and I—*

I took the one less traveled by,
And that has made all the difference.

"I feel as though Frost wrote that for me," I told Chappie. "I'm taking the road less traveled." He said he knew exactly what I meant.

When spring came, we went for long walks in the woods, searching for snakes.

Most wonderful of all was discovering that Chappie was also a photographer. He took highly technical pictures—fascinating photographs of wedge-shaped steel particles fusing under high heat. His developing and printing skills were much better than mine, and we began to work together in the darkroom. Then we started going out with our cameras and taking photographs together.

When Chappie was accepted into the graduate school in engineering and offered a teaching job, we celebrated by staying up all night to watch the sunrise. Chappie owned a dilapidated old automobile. The only reliable thing about it was the regularity with which it broke down, but mostly it got us where we wanted to go. We parked and climbed onto the hood to wait, and when the first bright rays shot above the purple horizon, we cheered.

I found in Chappie everything I had ever hoped for: a mix of my father's virtues of dedication and hard work, combined with a boyish kind of playfulness. He bought a kazoo and serenaded me. He hid silly notes around the darkroom for me to find. And when we went dancing, he would suddenly break into a tap routine.

I knew by the way he held me that Chappie longed for the closeness. But he was always a gentleman. I never had to stop his hands from roaming into dangerous territory. Eventually, to keep our passion in check, I told him we had to stop the ardent kisses. He agreed. There would be just one goodnight kiss, we decided, and not the long, lingering kind I yearned for but was afraid to allow. It wasn't easy, because we were always together.

Then, in May, Chappie told me he loved me. He belonged to me, he said, heart and soul. He had never been so sure of anything in his life. My own feelings were not so clear. I cared deeply for Chappie, but did that mean I was in love? I was only eighteen. I didn't feel ready to give myself completely to anyone. If I did, what would that mean for my dream of becoming a famous photographer and accomplishing great things?

When I tried to explain this to Chappie, he became upset. "Peggy," he declared, "I'm mad about you. I never believed I could love anyone as I love you. And I know how you feel. I know that you want to experience more of life before you settle down. It's important for you to finish your studies, and I must begin my career. I promise I'll wait for you for at least two years—even three, if it comes to that! And then you must promise you'll be mine for the rest of our lives!"

For the rest of our lives?

The world was spinning too fast. I felt confused. One minute I was happy, and the next I plunged into despair. Chappie complained that he couldn't concentrate. "Finals are coming up, and I have to focus on my studies, but all I can think about is *you*."

I didn't know how to respond to his pressure. And there was no one I could talk to. All the girls I knew had their sights set on marriage. Not one seemed to have any ambitions of her own.

◆◆

Toward the end of May my mother visited Ann Arbor for the first time. Naturally I wanted her to meet Chappie. He was anxious to meet her, too, he said, "But without you there, Peg. I want your mother to get to know me on my own, so she can ask me whatever she wants."

The two of them went for a walk and were gone for about an hour. I waited nervously in the parlor at Betsy's while girls gathered around the piano and sang. After Chappie left, Mother and I went to have our supper in the cafeteria. I showed her the revolving door where Chappie and I first met. "It was the funniest thing! He kept me going around and around until I agreed to have a date with him."

Mother smiled indulgently. "And it seems you've been going around and around ever since."

I felt myself blush. "Yes, I guess I have."

"Chappie and I had a long talk," she said when we were halfway through our meal. "I can see that he's serious about you." She pushed a lima bean through the mashed potatoes. "He made an excellent impression on me. He assured me that he has led a clean life and has the greatest respect for you." She eyed me, waiting for my reaction.

I looked away. "Yes, it's true. We're very careful not to let things get out of hand."

"It's important to control your ardor before marriage," she said. "It's not easy. I suppose every couple goes through the same struggle. Your father and I did, and it was worth it. We were pure when we married."

The awkward conversation ended, and we didn't talk about Chappie again.

After she went home to New Jersey, I had a letter from her. "I can tell, just by hearing your voice," she wrote, "that you're in love with this delightful young man."

I read my mother's letter several times and decided to stop questioning myself. She was right—I *was* in love with Chappie. But I was also determined to realize my ambitions. Maybe I wouldn't be going into the wilds as part of a team of scientists, yet surely I could find a way to become a successful photographer. Surely I could have both a career and marriage. It didn't have to be either/or, did it?

Chappie and I would be separated for the summer—he'd be staying with his parents in Detroit where he had a summer job playing percussion in a dance band, and I was going back to Camp Agaming in Connecticut to earn money for the next term. The time apart would be good for us. I'd have a chance to think about how Chappie fit into my future plans.

◆◆

Before the end of the semester, Professor Ruthven called me into his office again. He was my faculty advisor, and I assumed we'd be discussing the courses I'd take in the fall. "You've done very well in my courses again this semester, Miss White," he began. "And I've been thinking about you a great deal. What are your plans for the summer?"

I told him about Camp Agaming, adding, "I hope to do something different this year. I'd like to teach nature studies to the children. It would be less demanding than the photography classes I taught last year."

"Mmm," he murmured, and out came the pipe, the tobacco pouch, and the match. I waited while he finished the ritual of tamping, lighting, puffing. "I have another idea for you. You've told me that you hope to become a writer as well as a photographer. Your papers are consistently clear and concise. You apparently have a rapport with young children, or the camp would not have invited you to return. Why not try your hand at writing nature stories for youngsters, and taking photographs to illustrate them? You might enjoy creating such a book, and I'm sure children would enjoy reading it. I'd be happy to help you find a publisher."

This was a new direction, something I'd never considered, but I quickly agreed and I left Professor Ruthven's office feeling as if I'd just taken the first giant step toward my future.

◆◆

When I went home to Bound Brook early in June, I found

our house in a state of upheaval. Mother had given up trying to sell insurance policies and planned to move with twelve-year-old Roger to Ohio. "I've always thought I'd make a good teacher, and I've decided to study Braille and become a teacher of the blind. There's an excellent training school in Cleveland. I've already enrolled."

She hadn't said anything about this when she was in Ann Arbor, but when Mother made up her mind to do something, she did it. "I've found a duplex near the two universities. We'll live on the second floor and rent out the first floor to students, and that will help cover our expenses. There's even a room for you and Ruth when you come to visit."

It was painful to see our home dismantled, most of the furniture sold, the garden neglected. There were only pale rectangles on the walls where Father's photographs had once hung. After a week of helping Mother prepare for the move, I left for Camp Agaming to start setting up a darkroom for my students. As it turned out, I would teach photography *and* nature studies, but I would not be taking pictures of the campers to sell as postcards. Instead, I would begin work on the book that Professor Ruthven had proposed.

I was happy that Madge Jacobson had also returned as a counselor. We hadn't seen each other since the previous summer, and she couldn't wait to tell me that she was head over heels in love with a boy from Yale. It was "Ben said this" and "Ben thinks that" until I wanted to scream. They planned to announce their engagement at Christmas and marry in two years, right after she graduated.

"So," I said, "no career plans then? You're a good student. You made almost straight A's, didn't you?"

Madge laughed. "I did, but I'm majoring in English, and I don't want to teach. I'm not really *driven*—not the way you are, Peg!"

Madge seemed so sure about her life; it was all laid out for her. Professor Ruthven had high hopes for my future—everyone who saw my photographs did, and I did, too. But I still wasn't sure what shape that future would take. And what was I going to do about Chappie?

12

Torn—1923

MY NINETEENTH BIRTHDAY CAME AND WENT IN JUNE. When I had time, I immersed myself in the nature book Professor Ruthven had suggested. To fire the imagination of an eight-year-old, intelligent and curious about the world, I created miniature stage sets with pebbles and bits of greenery and posed a series of insects—dragonflies, spiders, ladybugs, gently chloroformed to keep them still—while I made dozens of photographs. Then I wrote a story about each insect in a few simple paragraphs. It was not the same as writing a paper for one of my science courses, but I discovered a talent for making a story come to life.

Work on the project went well, my campers were lively and engaging, and I should have been content, but I was not. I couldn't sleep, and as the weeks passed, I was exhausted. My eyes were ringed with dark circles. Food had no taste, and I lost weight. I couldn't bear to be alone, yet being with other people irritated me. I'd never been like this before and couldn't understand why I was now.

I told myself that all I had to do was to get through the next few weeks. In the fall I would be back in Ann Arbor, Chappie would be there in graduate school, and I would keep working on my nature book. Everything would be fine!

But it wasn't fine now. Whenever I started a letter to Chappie, I burst into tears and tore it up. When he didn't hear from me, he called, and that just made it worse.

Madge, who was used to seeing me as the girl in charge of her life, now watched me turning into a wreck. "I think you should go to a doctor," she said. "I'm worried about you, Peg! You just don't seem like yourself."

"I don't *feel* like myself," I confessed, already teary.

I took Madge's advice and looked up a doctor in Litchfield. Madge drove me to his office in her yellow roadster. "I'll be right here when you come out," she promised. "We all feel blue sometimes. You'll be yourself again in no time."

Dr. Graham had a little gray mustache and a pointy beard. He was reassuringly grandfatherly as I recited my symptoms. He peered in my throat and ears and listened to my heart.

He laid aside his stethoscope. "I don't believe there is anything physically wrong with you," he said, "but you appear to be on the verge of a nervous breakdown. You are perhaps demanding too much of yourself, working too hard. Your brain is unable to tolerate that pressure, and your nerves are strained." He removed his glasses and slid them into the pocket of his white coat. "I advise you to refrain from all intellectual activity. Try to relax. Rest. Go for long walks. Drink tea in the afternoons. Do you swim? Swimming is beneficial to the nervous system."

I nodded, promising to do as he suggested.

Afterward, I climbed into Madge's roadster, slammed the door, and burst into wrenching sobs.

"Didn't he prescribe something for you?" Madge asked as we bounced along the bumpy road back to camp. "Some pill or tonic?"

"No," I sobbed and dug for my handkerchief. "Just swimming. Long walks. Afternoon tea. And he says I should relax. He doesn't seem to understand—I'd relax if I could."

The summer dragged on, and I dragged on with it. My little girls, some of whom had been Agaming campers the summer before, watched me warily. They must have noticed that I had changed. I no longer stayed up all night to develop their pictures, no longer took long hikes with my camera. I stopped working on the insect book. Madge kept things going for both of us, and I was grateful. At last the summer ended, the campers left for home, and I made plans to visit Mother and Roger in Cleveland before returning to Ann Arbor.

"You'll be fine, Peg," Madge said as she prepared to leave. "I'm sure you will. You know that Chappie is madly in love with you."

I *did* know that. And that was part of the problem. Maybe it was the whole problem.

◆◆

Mother's new home was on the second floor of a plain clapboard house, on a dreary street with a weedy patch of a front yard, so unlike the unusual house and lush garden Father had created. University students had not yet returned, and the downstairs apartment sat vacant with a FOR RENT sign in the window of the sun porch.

I had been there for three days when Chappie called to ask if he could visit.

"Chappie's coming," I told my mother.

Mother was pleased. He had made a good impression on her, as he did on everyone. "Chappie reminds me of your father," she said wistfully. She didn't say so, but I knew she thought he would be an excellent husband.

Thinking about the visit made me feel queasy. None of Dr.

Graham's recommendations had done me a scrap of good. No matter how many long walks I took and how much tea I drank, I was still miserable. I didn't want Chappie to see how tired I looked, how nervous I seemed, how thin I had become. I didn't want him to see how easily I burst into tears. Nevertheless, on the day he was expected, I tried hard to pull myself together, put on one of my nice dresses, and fix my hair.

I was watching from the window when his old car pulled up in front of the house. He stepped out and adjusted a panama hat— I'd never seen him wear one, and somehow he looked different. Like a stranger. He straightened his tie. Then he came striding up the crumbling sidewalk and rang the bell marked "M. White."

I knew I should go down and greet him, but I felt paralyzed. Mother came out of the tiny kitchen, wiping her hands on a dishtowel, and glanced at me. "Aren't you going to let him in?" I shook my head. She sighed and hurried down to open the door.

Their voices sounded cheery as they climbed the narrow stairs together. My mouth was dry as dust, but I forced myself to smile when Chappie appeared at the sitting room door and hesitated, and I saw the shock and dismay in his eyes. Then he swooped in and gathered me in his arms, murmuring, "Darling, I've missed you so much!"

I could not bring myself to respond. I backed away. I opened my mouth and tried to speak, but nothing came out. Every ounce of strength had drained out of me.

Mother stepped in. "Margaret has been a little overwrought lately," she said in a bright voice that sounded entirely false. "Let's give her a chance to rest, and you and I can have a cup of tea and a nice chat."

She steered me back to the spare bedroom, scarcely larger than a closet, and eased me down onto the bed. "Rest," she said, throwing a quilt over me. "But not too long. I'll keep Chappie entertained for a while, but you must come out sooner or later."

I stared at the ceiling until Mother poked her head in to tell me that supper was on the table. I got up, straightened my clothes, and walked unsteadily to the little nook by the kitchen. Mother had set the table with her good china. Chappie pulled out my chair. The table was so small that our knees touched. There had been a time when that kind of closeness would have thrilled me. Now it frightened me. I could not utter more than a word or two, "please" and "thank you" and "no more," and finally, before the meal was over, "excuse me." I crept back to the stifling little bedroom, lay down, and wept.

The voices of Chappie and Mother continued for a while, and then I didn't hear Chappie's any more. The old Dodge coughed and started up under my window. My mother sat by my bedside, not saying anything, asking no questions, just sitting there in silence. Eventually I slept. The next day she said that Chappie had told her he loved me and wanted to marry me, and that he was prepared to wait as long as necessary.

"He said he was going on to Ann Arbor, and he will see you when you return for classes," Mother said. "He's sure that whatever is bothering you is temporary and will soon pass."

But it wasn't temporary, and it didn't pass. It just went underground.

Indecision—1923

SOMEHOW I PULLED MYSELF TOGETHER AND WENT back to Ann Arbor for the fall semester, plunging into my science courses and my photography. The Mungers had again covered my tuition and basic expenses, so although I had very little spending money, at least I didn't have to worry about staying in school.

Chappie and I were constantly together, often going out to take pictures for the *'Ensian*. He liked to catch people in action—playing ball, for instance. But people didn't interest me as much as the small details that escaped nearly everyone else's notice: an unusual lock on a gate, or the reflection on a coffee urn. We photographed campus buildings and wandered through the neighborhoods of Ann Arbor in search of other unusual shots. Chappie told me, over and over, "Peg, you have the eye of an artist. You see things in a way no one else does." But he was a genius in the darkroom, and we developed and printed our pictures together.

The editor of the *'Ensian* asked me to take on the job of picture editor, but I turned it down. I wanted to make photographs, not pick which ones to use. Since Chappie was serving on the advisory board of the *'Ensian*, plus taking pictures for a school magazine and the Ann Arbor newspaper, I took over most of the darkroom work, developing and printing his pictures as well as mine. All this in addition to my classes. Sometimes I thought about the nature book I had started and then abandoned, but there was no time for that.

And then there was my love for Chappie. The worst of my symptoms had disappeared as mysteriously as they had arrived. My appetite came back and I began to sleep again, but nothing was resolved. Is it possible to be both happy and miserable at the same time?

Chappie and I talked a lot about what our lives would be like when we were married, and I sometimes pictured myself in the middle of that domestic scene, our two sons and two daughters running to greet their papa when he came home from work while I tended a pot roast on the stove. But other times I imagined myself on a grand adventure, exploring some faraway place with my camera. Chappie was nowhere in the picture. Back and forth I swung, unable to feel comfortable with either picture.

Chappie pressed me to make up my mind. I could not. The more I leaned one way and then the other, the more morose, peevish, and sullen he became. He apologized: he didn't want his wretched moods to affect mine. Naturally, they did. At times he threatened to break off our relationship. If he couldn't have all of me, then he would have none. He refused to speak to me for days, or else we argued. I lashed out, and it was my turn to apologize. We wept in each other's arms, swore our love, tried to be kinder to each other.

Then we started all over again. We were going nowhere.

I sank back into depression, unable to eat or sleep. There was no one to confide in. Ruth was in Boston. Mother had witnessed my despair, and she struggled to make sense of it. Finally she wrote, urging me to see a psychiatrist. "You must not continue in your misery. It will destroy you."

The Litchfield doctor's prescription—to give my mind a rest—had been impossible to follow. It was as if he had told me to give my lungs a rest by not breathing. What could a psychiatrist do?

But when I could not stand it any longer, I took Mother's advice. I asked the nurse at the campus infirmary to recommend a psychiatrist. She looked at me oddly, but she wrote a name and address on a slip of paper and handed it to me without a word.

I stood outside his door, staring at the name on the shingle—Wesley D. Stansfield, MD—and trying to work up my courage. I hesitated so long that I nearly missed the appointment. Dr. Stansfield was thin and bald with saggy little pouches under his eyes, and he wore a pince-nez. His barren office was furnished with a chair, a couch, and a row of framed diplomas printed in Latin.

"Now tell me, Miss White, why have you come to see me?"

I began to cry. Dr. Stansfield waited until I stopped and then asked me why I was crying.

"Because I'm miserable!" I wailed.

"And why are you miserable?"

"Because I can't make up my mind what I want."

"What do you see as your choices?"

Haltingly, I talked about my love for Chappie and my conflicting desire to make a name for myself. The psychiatrist listened, sometimes asking a question, and gave me an appointment to come back in a week. Every Wednesday for two months I recounted the incidents during the previous week that upset me. Nothing changed. Then I decided that I'd marry Chappie in three years. But the decision only made things worse. I was still miserable. Perhaps I could not be cured.

One Wednesday Dr. Stansfield asked me to describe my childhood.

I gave him a glowing account of my walks with Father, the stories he'd told me, the snakes we'd brought home, the caterpillars we'd watched changing into butterflies. I described the high standards set for me by my mother. "'The hard way is always the better way,' she always told me."

"So, you admired your demanding mother and perhaps idolized your father?"

"Oh, yes! I've never known anyone like him!" I listed my reasons: his dedication to his work, his genius, his love of nature, his passion for photography.

"Ah, so perhaps your father was perfect! And Chappie can never measure up!"

My reaction was immediate. I blurted out the words I had never spoken or even allowed myself to *think*: "But my father was Jewish!"

There it was. I had given away our secret, said what Mother had warned me not to say. Jewishness had been the basic flaw in Father's character, the one thing my mother could not forgive.

The psychiatrist regarded me calmly, his expression neutral. "It bothers you that your father was a Jew?"

I stared at my hands, clenched in my lap. I couldn't bear to look at him. "Yes," I admitted. "I suppose it does. My mother dislikes Jews. Many people do. And I'm half Jewish!"

Dr. Stansfield did not appear to be shocked. "Are you afraid that others would reject you if they knew you have Jewish blood running through your veins?"

"Yes," I whispered. I buried my face in my hands.

"And what about you, Miss White? Do you also dislike Jews?"

"I—I don't know!"

"You mentioned your father's family. How do you feel about them?"

I had to regain my composure before I could answer. "My father's brother, Uncle Lazar, is very kind. He's helping to pay for my education. I don't know my cousins very well. I've spent so little time with them, because my mother dislikes them so much."

"Do you know why she dislikes them?"

"She says they're like all Jews and think they're better than anyone else. I guess I never questioned that."

"I believe that we may have learned something important here today," said the doctor, scribbling notes on a pad. "We have perhaps discovered the source of your inner turmoil. You have kept this secret for a very long time, is that not so?"

I nodded. "Since just after Father died almost two years ago. Mother told us then. I had no idea before that."

"You've kept your secret even from your friend Chappie?"

"Especially from Chappie! What if I lose him because of this—this flaw? You're the first person I've told, doctor."

"And how do you feel, now that you have told the first person? And that person has not turned away from you, or made you feel worthless?"

I considered his question, and then I admitted—first to myself, and then to the doctor—that I felt relieved.

"Doesn't it seem likely that Chappie will not turn away when you share your deepest secret with him? And that perhaps your self-doubt has clouded your ability to make decisions about what is important in your life?"

I didn't see how revealing my secret would solve the other problems, but I agreed to tell Chappie.

The next day we went for a long walk in the countryside. The day was bright and clear, and the leaves that had changed color weeks earlier had drifted down around us. Chappie watched me warily, as though he expected me to begin sobbing for no apparent reason, as I often had in the past weeks.

I gathered my courage and grabbed his hand. "Chappie, I have something to tell you," I said, struggling to keep my voice steady. "There is a secret in my family, something I think you should know. My father was a Jew, and so I'm half Jewish. I've been afraid to tell you, because I didn't want your feelings for me to change."

Lately Chappie had seemed afraid even to touch me, fearing that might set off another storm of tears. But now he turned to face me. "Peggy, my darling girl! How could you ever believe that something like that would make me feel any differently about you? For one thing, being Jewish isn't a cause for shame. For another, I love you so deeply that nothing you tell me will ever change that." He kissed me passionately, and I returned his kisses with more fervor than I had felt in months.

◆◆

But even then, as autumn faded and the unforgiving Michigan winter closed in, my uneasiness did not disappear. Confessing hadn't cured me. I worried about money, and so did Chappie, who earned extra income playing in local dance bands. Even with help from Uncle Lazar and the Mungers, my budget was painfully tight. I moved out of the residence hall and into a cheap boarding house. When the snows melted and spring came, Chappie and I set up a show in the library of pictures we'd taken around campus in the different seasons, hoping to make money. We sold them all, for as much as a dollar-fifty apiece, and took orders for more.

We were talking again about marriage. I was still uncertain. If I could find time to finish the nature book I'd started in summer and it sold well, maybe I'd be asked to create other books. I knew my photographs were good, and I wanted to explore every possibility. If I settled into the conventional kind of marriage Chappie expected and the only kind I knew, how would I ever become recognized—famous, even—for my talent?

I told him I thought we should wait three years. But we were passionately in love, and we both wondered how we could possibly wait that long.

Chappie was offered a teaching position at Purdue University in Indiana, far from Ann Arbor. Of course he accepted, but now it was clear I would have to make up my mind. Go with Chappie to Indiana, or stay in Michigan and finish my degree? Marry now, marry later, or not marry at all?

The more I wavered, the more Chappie's impatience grew. He wanted me with him all the time, and when I tried to go off and do things on my own, he became unreasonable and possessive. He pouted like a child if I so much as spoke to another man, so jealous that he wept. And sometimes he shouted at me, "Why can't you be like other girls and just want to get married? What's so hard about that?"

When I told him the truth—"Because I'm afraid of losing who I am and what I want to do with my life"—he replied caustically, "Maybe you should talk to that psychiatrist again."

But none of this diminished our intense physical longing for each other. By the end of the term, with the prospect of a long, hot summer ahead, we could hardly stand to be apart. And so I made my decision. We would get married, and we would do it now.

14

Love and Marriage—1924

WE PICKED THE DATE FOR OUR WEDDING: FRIDAY, the thirteenth of June. We would fly in the face of superstition, thumb our noses at the notion of bad luck! The thirteenth was also the day before my twentieth birthday.

It would be *very* small, with only a handful of people—our parents and three girls from my boarding house who had become my friends.

Braced for Mother's disapproval, I called to tell her our plans.

"Oh, Margaret, you're so young!" she sighed. "I did so hope you'd complete your education first."

"I'm going to get my degree," I assured her. "Chappie promises that I can. We're both hoping you'll come to our wedding."

"Well, I know how much you love him," she said, "and you do have my approval. But I simply do not have the means to travel all the way to Michigan. Train tickets for your brother and me are more than I can afford . . ."

"It's all right, Mother," I said. "We'll send you pictures."

That conversation was easier than I'd expected.

Chappie thought we should make a quick trip to Detroit.

"I want you to meet Momma," he said. "She'll be upset if she hasn't had a chance to get to know you before we're married."

This was just before final examinations—not a good time to be making a trip, even one of less than fifty miles, in an auto as chronically unreliable as Chappie's ancient Dodge. Nevertheless, we were going. "We'll stay for lunch and then drive straight back to Ann Arbor," Chappie promised.

Late on a hot and humid Saturday morning we arrived at an unremarkable house in a neighborhood of ordinary houses with neat front yards. This was where Chappie and his sister, Marian, had grown up. I was wearing one of my Munger-sponsored dresses, and it clung uncomfortably to my perspiring body.

"What have you told them about me?" I asked.

"That you are the love of my life, the most beautiful girl in the world and also the smartest, and that I'm marrying you in two weeks minus one day." He grabbed my hand and we hurried up the steps.

Chappie's father, Everett Chapman Sr., a slight, bald man with pale blue eyes and a thin smile, opened the door. "Glad to meet you," he said and offered a weak handshake. "Come in, come in."

We stepped into a narrow hall crowded with dark, brooding pictures in ornate frames, and Mrs. Chapman made her entrance. Tall and elegant, almost regal, with onyx eyes and a porcelain complexion, his mother wore her handsome silver hair in a crown of braids. It was clear where Chappie got his good looks. He introduced me. "Momma, this is Margaret."

"So," she said, looking me over coolly, "you're the girl who has stolen my son."

How should I have responded to such a greeting? I glanced at Chappie, hoping—expecting—that he would smooth things over, but he didn't say a word.

"How was your drive over?" inquired Mr. Chapman, and he

and Chappie got into a conversation about problems with the old Dodge.

Mrs. Chapman interrupted to say that *their* vehicle was ready for the scrap heap but they couldn't possibly afford to replace it, and marched off toward the kitchen.

I offered to help, but she glared at me and replied shortly, "No *thank you*, Miss White."

When Mrs. Chapman announced that luncheon was ready, we went into a dining room darkened by heavy drapery. I poked at the tomato aspic and watched the lemon sherbet melt in my dish while the Chapmans complained that their next-door neighbors had just ordered new furniture, the people across the street were letting the weeds take over their front lawn, and someone else's dog barked at all hours.

"We certainly could use your financial help, Everett," his mother said, adding pointedly, "but apparently you've made other plans."

I, of course, was responsible for the "other plans." I tried hard to find something to like about Chappie's mother, but so far was finding it impossible. I thought Chappie would say something to make her see that we were truly in love and that nothing would interfere with our plans, but again he remained silent, and that bothered me.

"I'm sure you made a wonderful impression," Chappie said when we were finally on our way back to Ann Arbor. Was he blind, or was he lying? Mrs. Chapman had disliked me on sight, and Mr. Chapman's opinion, if he had one, didn't matter.

For the next two weeks Chappie's mother pressed her campaign to make him feel guilty. "Momma says I'm thinking of no one but myself," he confessed. "She says that my first responsibility is to them, and Poppa seems to agree. They assume I'll be able to support them, now that I've taken a job at Purdue."

"They expect you to support them? Your father is unable to work?"

"He works as a salesman, but he doesn't earn enough money to give Momma the things she feels she deserves."

"But you're just starting out! You have no money! We can barely support ourselves, let alone your parents. Do they understand that?"

Chappie shrugged. "I don't believe they want to understand it. They've told me I'm being very selfish." His mother's campaign was succeeding.

"They'll get over it," I said, trying to make him feel better. "They're just not ready to see their boy get married."

◆◆

Neither of us had any idea how to plan a wedding. Luckily for us, Chappie had a close friend, Arthur Moore, a professor of electrical engineering only a few years older than him. Arthur's wife, Jo, loved the idea of having the wedding ceremony in their house.

"Don't you worry, Peggy," she said. "We'll figure everything out. You'll have a wedding you'll remember for the rest of your lives."

She would bake a nice cake, she promised. Her garden was in full bloom, so I could have roses for my bouquet. That was another stroke of good luck, because Chappie and I had barely two nickels to rub together.

What was I going to wear? I had the clothes that the Mungers had financed for me, but I didn't own anything that qualified as a wedding dress, and I didn't think it was proper to take advantage of the Mungers' generosity to spend money on something so frivolous. I asked for Jo's advice.

"I was in a wedding party just last year," Jo said, "and I wore a blue dress that I think would look very pretty on you. We're about the same size."

So that issue was settled.

But Chappie had definite ideas for my wedding ring. "I'll make it for you myself," Chappie said. This was a side of him I'd never seen, and I thought it was a terribly romantic idea.

With only a few days to go until the wedding, we made the rounds of jewelry shops in search of a gold nugget that he would transform into my ring. But every jeweler we visited tried to persuade us to buy a ring instead.

We decided to try just one more place, a tiny hole-in-the-wall. The wizened old owner disappeared into his back room and returned with a tray of gold teeth and other odds and ends. He watched suspiciously as we poked through the collection until three nuggets caught our eye. Each was a slightly different color—yellow, white, and reddish gold.

"There they are," Chappie announced, lining up the nuggets on a ragged scrap of velvet. "Perfect."

The shopkeeper weighed the three nuggets. Chappie paid for them and dropped them into his shirt pocket. "I'll begin work tonight."

The day before the wedding Chappie telephoned me at my boarding house. "The ring is ready," he said, and I could hear the excitement in his voice. "Let's make sure it fits."

Chappie had fashioned the nuggets into a lovely circlet. The ring lay gleaming on the anvil, and as I reached for it, Chappie said, "No, wait—let me give it a few more taps, to make sure it's perfectly round."

He tapped it once with a tiny hammer, and the ring broke into two pieces. I began to cry, and Chappie held me, murmuring, "Don't worry, Peg. I'll make it over again, and it will be stronger than ever."

"But it won't be ready for the ceremony tomorrow!"

"It's not a catastrophe, Peg," Chappie said, stroking my hair. "We'll use some other ring, and it will be all right."

That evening Chappie's parents arrived in Ann Arbor, and Mrs. Chapman announced their plans to have dinner with their son. I was not invited. Chappie made no objection, and again I swallowed my anger—at him as well as his mother. But I was glad not to be around Mrs. Chapman more than I absolutely had to.

My friends from Betsy's—Alice, Helen, and Middie—invited me to my last dinner as a single girl. They had chipped in to buy me a gift, a white nightgown adorned with yards of lace and satin ribbon.

"You won't have it on for long," Helen said, laughing. "But it's nice to have it, to make your official appearance as a bride on your wedding night."

I knew little about weddings, and the more I heard, the more I wondered if it wouldn't be better if Chappie and I sneaked off to a justice of the peace. Then I wouldn't have to endure his mother the next day. She had already informed Chappie that she wished me to call her "Mother Chapman." I thought "Duchess of Detroit" suited her much better.

"What about a honeymoon?" Middie asked. "Or is that a secret?"

"We're going to the Chapman family cottage on a lake." That had been Mother Chapman's idea. Chappie insisted that I'd love the place, and we didn't have the money to go anywhere else.

"Oh, Peggy, it sounds so romantic!" Alice sighed. "Just think, tomorrow night this time, you'll be Mrs. Everett Chapman, and you'll be on your honeymoon!"

◆ ◆

Jo Moore had arranged flowers and greenery in front of the fireplace where we would exchange our vows at eleven o'clock. I wore Jo's blue crepe dress with a flounced skirt. She loaned me elbow-length white gloves and a pair of shoes and made me a gift of a pair of silk stockings. And she took the wedding ring off her own finger and handed it to Chappie, whispering, "Remember to give it back to me after the ceremony!"

Somewhere Arthur Moore found a minister to perform the ceremony. The man was dreadful, loudly prompting us through every line of our vows as though we were deaf. He had scarcely finished blaring the opening lines, "Dearly beloved, we are gathered here today in the sight of God," when I heard a moaning sob behind me. Mrs. Chapman was weeping as though her son had just died. To her, I suppose, it must have seemed like it. She keened so noisily that the minister raised the volume another notch to shout over her.

We stumbled through our vows, the minister pronounced us man and wife, and Chappie planted a dutiful kiss on my cheek. Arthur was the first to offer hearty congratulations, and Jo rushed off to ladle cups of strawberry punch and pass around egg salad sandwiches and then to coach us as we cut the cake. Mrs. Chapman continued to honk into her handkerchief, and Chappie's father hovered nearby lest she keel over in a dead faint. I secretly hoped she would.

We got away as soon as we could. I changed out of Jo's blue dress and into my everyday clothes, and Middie and Alice and Helen tossed handfuls of rice at us as we jumped into the Dodge. My friends had lettered *JUST MARRIED* on the rear window and tied a couple of tin cans to the bumper.

Nobody remembered to take pictures.

15

Honeymoon—1924

BEFORE OUR HONEYMOON COULD BEGIN, CHAPPIE and I drove to the darkroom to print the photographs of the campus we'd shown in the library and for which we had a backlog of orders. That night, Friday the thirteenth, we slept in Chappie's rented room. Exhausted, I forgot all about my white bridal nightgown.

Saturday, my twentieth birthday, we were up early and back in the darkroom. We had been hired to take photographs at commencement exercises at the university on Sunday, and for the next few days we spent practically every minute in the darkroom, developing and printing. We had been married for a week before we were able to leave on our honeymoon.

The Chapmans' cottage was on one of the lakes seventeen miles north of Ann Arbor. The Dodge died twice along the unpaved road before we arrived. Late afternoon sunlight filtered through the tall trees surrounding the cottage and reflected on the water. Sailboats drifted around little islands dotted with green trees and white rocks. The cottage itself was dark and dank. We threw open the windows, knocked down cobwebs, and cleaned mouse droppings off the scarred oak table. We found sheets and moth-eaten blankets in a musty cupboard and made up the rickety bed with a tired mattress that sagged in the middle. I was never much good at housekeeping, but I rose to the occasion at least this once.

By evening the cabin was habitable. Chappie lit the kerosene lamp and fired up the wood stove. Jo Moore had packed a hamper with supplies she thought we'd need and Arthur had delivered it to Chappie's boarding house before we left—neither of us would have thought to pick up groceries—and I scrambled some eggs and brewed a pot of coffee. We were alone, in love, eager to start our married life together.

But we weren't alone for long.

After two blissful nights and one lazy day spent paddling a leaky canoe along the shore and swimming in the still-frigid waters, we were startled to hear an auto crunching down the gravel path. "Yoohoo!" caroled the familiar voice of Mrs. Chapman.

"It's your mother," I said, peering out the window. "And she's not alone. There's a girl with her. Can we pretend we're not here?"

The girl was Marian, Chappie's sister. I had heard a little about her but had not met her.

"We decided we could do with a short vacation," Mrs. Chapman announced brightly. "Marian has been having such a difficult time, and as long as you're here, we thought we'd join you for a nice family visit. Everett, dear, go bring our luggage from the car."

There was no explanation of Marian's "difficult time," but Everett Dear did as Momma ordered. I realized from the amount of their luggage that this was not going to be an overnight visit. Soon our uninvited guests were settled into the bedroom next to ours, and the Duchess of Detroit was waiting to be served.

"Marian and I would love some coffee, Margaret. Or is it Peg?

Or Peggy? Or Maggie?" She cocked her head to one side. "You seem like a Maggie to me."

"You may call me whatever you like, *Mother* Chapman," I said evenly, trying to keep the sarcasm out of my voice. "Chappie calls me Peggy."

"All right, then, *Peggy*," she said, as though the name had an unpleasant taste. "But please don't call my son 'Chappie.' I named him Everett, and that is what I wish to hear him called."

"Of course," I said, gritting my teeth. My mother also disapproved of nicknames, but she never lectured my friends.

Puffy-eyed Marian sat sullenly at the kitchen table, her head in her hands. Marian's marriage had come to a bitter end, her mother announced.

"I've done nothing but cry for the past week," Marian said, and began to sob again.

Women in my family hardly ever cried, at least not in front of other people. This seemed to be a family of theatrical weepers, and it made me uncomfortable.

"Nobody loves me!" Marian wailed. "Not one single person! I have nothing to live for!"

"Certainly you do, dear," Mrs. Chapman said, patting Marian's shoulder. "I, on the other hand, have nothing but woes!"

Chappie had been standing close to me, his arm around my waist, but when Marian gazed tearfully at us, his arm dropped and he moved away. "I think the coffee is ready," he said. It felt like a chilly breeze blowing between us.

I retrieved four cups from the cupboard and poured cream into a pitcher with a broken handle. Chappie pulled out a chair for his mother at the table. I pulled out my own chair, helped myself to coffee, and reached for the cream pitcher.

"Don't use too much of it, Peggy," Mrs. Chapman warned. "We don't want to run out. I absolutely cannot drink coffee if it doesn't have enough cream in it. I hope you have more, and plenty of ice for the icebox, too. If not, Everett can drive into the village and pick up a block. We're going to need more groceries. I'll make a list."

I made a show of adding only a few drops to my cup. Mrs. Chapman took the pitcher and turned her coffee nearly white. And just like that, I moved from disliking my new mother-in-law to detesting her.

"Let me tell you what's happened," she said. "The neighbors have completely refurnished their house. Besides the loveseat and matching chairs, they've bought a mahogany dining room table and a china closet, an Oriental rug, and probably even more things I haven't seen yet. Can you imagine how that makes me feel? Your father and I, existing in such dismal circumstances that I am denied the finer things of life?"

Chappie shifted uneasily in his chair. "I'm sorry to hear that, Momma. But Poppa did buy you the davenport you wanted."

I stirred a spoonful of sugar into my coffee, wishing I could sneak something into Momma's cup to put her into a deep coma. What a dreadful woman! And why did Chappie just *sit* there, taking it, looking like a whipped dog?

"Yes, you're sorry! I'm sure you're very sorry indeed! And a cheap davenport it is, too—not at all what I had in mind." Her voice rose shrilly. "But it is your duty as my son to come to our aid! Don't we deserve better?"

"Yes, Momma," Chappie murmured.

"I'm glad you understand that, Everett," Mrs. Chapman said. "Now we'll see if you're as good as your word."

How could he put up with this? I felt completely helpless. It was awfully clear that Chappie was not going to tell her that it was not his responsibility. The walls of the cottage were so thin that, at night, we lay rigidly side by side, not touching, and listened to his mother's stentorian snores and his sister's muffled sobs in the next room. I wondered what it would take to get them to leave.

❖❖

On a Friday morning two weeks after we were married and five days after his mother and sister arrived to share our honeymoon, Chappie got up early and left the cottage without waking me. He had work to do in his laboratory, and I knew that he would not be back until late that night. He played in a dance band in Ann Arbor to earn extra money, and his Friday nights were always busy. After he'd gone, I was awakened by a loud thumping and sloshing in the kitchen. My dear mother-in-law was cleaning, and my first thought was to ignore it. My second thought was to climb out of bed, get dressed in a hurry, and volunteer to help.

"Well, Peggy," said Mrs. Chapman when I appeared in the doorway, "is it your usual habit to sleep away the best part of the day while others work?"

And where was poor Marian, I wondered? Shouldn't she be up and helping, too?

But determined to ignore this opening shot, I greeted her cheerfully. "Good morning, Mother Chapman. What would you like me to do?"

"Start by washing the windows," she said. "A person can scarcely see through them."

I found a bucket and filled it at the pump in the sink. After doing a couple of windows, a dozen small panes in each, I'd fix myself some breakfast. Then I'd ask Mrs. Chapman to join me for a cup of coffee. Maybe I could begin to make some kind of peace if her boy wasn't there to be her audience. If she got to know me, she might realize that I was a likable person.

I was wiping a glass pane with a chamois when Mrs. Chapman paused in her furious scrubbing and called out from the kitchen, "Tell me, Peggy, what did your mother think when you announced your plans to marry?"

I rinsed the chamois in the bucket and moved on to the next pane before I answered. "She was worried at first because she thought we were too young. She agrees that it's important for me to finish my courses and graduate. But when she realized how much in love we are, she changed her mind and gave her approval. She's happy for us."

"Really? I'm certainly glad *someone* is happy! Your mother has gained a son, and I've lost a son. I do congratulate you, but I never want to see you again."

Had I heard her correctly? *I never want to see you again.* Nobody would dare say such a cruel thing to another person! Angry and shaken, I clutched the damp chamois, unsure what to do next. Scarcely able to think—certainly not clearly—I slipped out the front door of the cottage, closing it quietly behind me. I had to find Chappie and tell him exactly what had happened. Surely my husband would finally stand up to his mother and make things right!

I made my way up the gravel path to the road and started walking. I knew it was seventeen miles to Ann Arbor, but I didn't think about the distance. The morning was still pleasantly cool. After about a mile, my head cleared and I realized that I had left without my purse. I had also neglected to eat any breakfast.

There was no turning back. *I never want to see you again.*

I kept walking. The sun rose higher, the patches of shade shrank, and I was growing hungrier. Occasionally an automobile rumbled by on the dusty road, and the driver glanced at me curiously. I thought of sticking out my thumb and asking for a ride, but I was too embarrassed. There would be questions, and I didn't want to answer them.

I plodded on, plagued by blackflies and gnats. The sun blazed directly overhead. My feet were blistering. I came to a filling station and stopped for a drink of water. "Hot enough for ya?" the attendant inquired, eyeing me, and I nodded. I might have asked for help, but pride would not let me. I rested for a while and then continued my journey.

In mid-afternoon I reached the outskirts of Ann Arbor. The streetcar line ended here, and if I'd had a nickel in my pocket I might have ridden the last couple of miles into town. The sun was still high when I stumbled up the street to Arthur and Jo Moore's home. I knew that I looked a fright, but I was past caring. I knocked on the door and got no answer. Exhausted, I sank into a chair on their front porch to wait. Hours passed—I had no idea how many. I had not eaten all day, and I was dizzy with hunger, but I had nowhere else to go. Sunset came. Lights began to flicker on in houses up and down the street, but there was no sign of the Moores.

At last a pair of headlamps swung into the driveway, and I levered myself up from the chair where I'd been dozing. Arthur saw me first and leaped out of the car. "Peggy!" he cried. "What on earth?"

I threw myself into Jo's arms, sobbing. "Oh, you poor dear!" she murmured, and turned to Arthur. "Let's get her inside. We can ask questions later."

The two half-carried me into the house, washed my face as though I were a small child, gave me water and then weak tea, and decided that a soft-boiled egg and toast would be just the thing. While I ate, I described my conversation with Mrs. Chapman. "'I never want to see you again.' She actually said that."

I saw the look the Moores exchanged—they had witnessed her behavior at the wedding. Now they had a hurried conference: Chappie would be playing for another couple of hours before heading back to the lake. Arthur would find him and bring him to their home.

"Meanwhile, dear child, you must rest," Jo said firmly. "Shall I fix you another egg? How about a whole wheat muffin with some marmalade?"

◆◆

I was asleep in the Moores' guest room when Chappie arrived sometime after midnight. Drowsily I reached up to draw him close, but after some tearful kisses and before I had a chance to tell him what his mother had said to me, he pulled away. "I can't stay here, Peg. I have to drive to the cottage. Momma will be so worried if I don't. We'll have plenty of time to talk tomorrow."

"Go, then," I told him and turned my face to the wall.

He came back at noon, bringing our clothes and the news that his mother and Marian were returning to Detroit. I had slept most of the morning and taken a long, hot bath, and I was sitting on the Moores' back terrace in Jo's dressing gown. My filthy clothes had been washed and hung out to dry. Arthur and Jo had been discreet in their questions, but Chappie wanted an explanation.

"Peggy, what happened?" he asked, pulling up a chair beside me. "Momma said that you became hysterical over some trivial thing and ran off. She said she couldn't imagine what would have caused you to do that. She thought you'd just gone down to the lake to get control of yourself."

I stared at Chappie for a moment and then looked away. If I told him the truth, repeated the cruel words his mother had flung at me, would he even believe me? I doubted it. Better, then, to say nothing. "Yes," I said quietly. "Of course. She was right."

"Darling," Chappie said sympathetically, his hand on my knee, "I wonder if it might be a good idea for you to have another talk with Dr. Stansfield. He was so helpful to you—"

I cut him off before he could say any more. "You think I'm crazy! Your mother has convinced you that there's something wrong with me! Well, I can assure you there is not." I brushed his hand away and stood up, tightening the sash on the dressing gown. "Your mother has made it perfectly clear that she dislikes me and that she disapproves of our marriage. Yes, I behaved irrationally! I should have remembered to take my purse—that was my main mistake. I do apologize for the trouble I've caused Arthur and Jo and you, because I know you were worried. I doubt that your mother gave my absence a second thought." I started toward the door. "I'm going to dress. Then let's go home."

Home was Chappie's boarding house. His room was too small for both of us, so I had taken a room down the hall. It was awkward, but it was supposed to be temporary. In a few weeks we'd be moving to Indiana. We'd have a regular home of our own, I would be in my fourth year of college, and Mrs. Chapman would be out of our lives.

Except she wasn't. It didn't matter that she was three hundred miles away in Detroit.

The flow of letters grew from a stream to a flood, and the story never changed: everything was wrong in her life, and it was all Chappie's fault. She was a damsel in distress, he was supposed to be her knight in shining armor, and he'd failed her. She could never be happy, she told him. It would be better if she didn't love him so much. Someday he would understand what he had done to her, but by then it would be too late!

Mr. Chapman made things even worse, warning Chappie that if he didn't write to his mother at least once a week, he would have to accept responsibility for whatever became of her. His father predicted it would be dire.

The Chapmans made sure I understood that I was at the root of all this misery.

Starting Over—1925

BY THE END OF 1924—WE HAD BEEN MARRIED ONLY six months—I was often thinking how much better my life would be if I weren't Mrs. Margaret Chapman. Even the name upset me. I had been Margaret White all my life, and I had wanted my name to become famous. My own name—not my husband's. I felt as if I were losing my identity. And my marriage seemed to be falling apart.

I scarcely knew who I was anymore. I had not worked on my children's book about insects for months. I had taken all of Professor Ruthven's courses, and without him to guide and inspire me, my interest shifted from herpetology to paleontology, from snakes to fossils. It was a drastic change, and it meant that in my fourth year of college, instead of being a senior at Purdue, I had to start over as a freshman and take a different set of required courses. The girls in my classes were close to my age, but we had nothing in common. They chattered about their dates, the dances and parties to which they'd been invited, and the clothes they planned to wear, just as I had only a couple of years earlier. When I told them I was married, the wife of a faculty member, they shied away. The other faculty wives were no better match—I was decades younger than any of them, sometimes even younger than their own daughters.

At a dinner for faculty and their wives, I was seated next to a gray-haired matron who assumed that I, too, must be a professor's daughter. She asked what I was studying, and I told her.

"A scientist in the making!" she enthused. "How nice. Well, I enjoy doing needlepoint," she said and described the cushions she'd worked to raise money for a charity. "What are your hobbies, dear? Besides collecting rocks, or whatever it is paleontologists do?" she asked.

"I enjoy taking photographs." How bland that sounded!

What had once been my passion was now reduced to little more than a hobby. Had this really happened to me? I felt sick just saying it: *I enjoy taking photographs.*

The woman nodded approvingly. She was the advisor to a campus sorority, she said, and her girls were looking for someone to take pictures for a book they were putting together. "Portraits of the girls, informal pictures of life in the sorority house, that sort of thing. I'd be pleased to recommend you for the job, Peggy."

"That sort of thing" was not the kind of photography I loved to do; there was no artistry in it, no imagination required. But it was an opportunity to use my camera and earn a little money of my own. I leaped at the offer and spent hours taking pictures. It turned out to be a disaster. I didn't have enough experience in photographing people, and I misjudged the available light. I overexposed every single shot, and the pictures were worthless. I was horribly embarrassed and didn't get any more assignments. This failure was a crushing disappointment for me, but it didn't bother Chappie.

"It's my job to support you, Peg," he said sternly. "You should not be spending your time trying to earn money. Your job is to keep house."

To keep house! That remark chilled me, but I did not argue with him. We were arguing more and more, and to challenge him would have done no good.

◆◆

We had been married just a year when Chappie accepted a job with a company in Cleveland. We were moving again, and I was pleased. I could see my mother and Roger occasionally. Maybe the change would be good for both Chappie and me. Our marriage was in trouble, I knew that, but I hoped we could make a fresh start.

We rented a sunny little apartment on the top floor of an old house where I could set up a darkroom in the bathroom. I found a job teaching children at the Museum of Natural History. Then I signed up for evening classes in education at Western Reserve University. I thought my chances of finding steady employment as a teacher were probably good.

Cleveland was a much more interesting and energetic city than the sleepy Indiana town where Purdue was located. I explored the city with my camera. It was only when I was peering through the cracked lens of my secondhand Ica Reflex that I felt truly alive again. I wandered along the docks on Lake Erie and poked into the shops along Broadway, thinking I might put together a photographic essay of the city. But there were too many other demands on my time and energy, and I didn't follow through on my idea.

Housework bored me. Dirty dishes piled up in the bathtub—the kitchen sink was too small. Dirty laundry overflowed the hamper, and the cupboard went bare. I had to face Chappie's wrath when he came home and shouted that the place was no better than a pigpen, and it was my fault. Worse than his shouting was his complete silence. Sometimes he would not speak for days. It was as if I didn't exist. I could hardly believe this was the Chappie I had fallen in love with. What had happened to him?

And what was happening to *me*?

On my good days, when I was determined to prove that I was a capable wife, I cleaned and washed and ironed and prepared elaborate meals, trying to please my husband. On his good days, Chappie was sweet and loving. But often he sulked. Once he told me that he thought he hated me, although he wouldn't say why. Another time he bellowed, "Why would anyone choose to be married? I'm done with it! Finished!"

Later, when he was calm, he said he was sorry, he would try to be more patient, we must give our marriage another chance. I agreed. This was how it went, seesawing up and down, through a second year.

I began to quietly put aside a little money, imagining what my life might be like as a single woman. At the end of two years it was clear to me, as it must have been to Chappie that nothing was going to change, that our marriage was over.

In the summer of 1926, soon after my twenty-second birthday, I applied to Cornell University in upstate New York, and was accepted. I'd heard that Cornell had a good zoology department, and with my courses in herpetology and a brief detour into paleontology behind me, I would be able to graduate in a year. I'd also heard that there were waterfalls on the Cornell campus—Cascadilla Falls, Triphammer Falls, Forest Falls. Such picturesque names!

When I'd told Chappie that I wanted to leave—leave Cleveland, leave *him*—he'd reluctantly agreed. "Maybe it's for the best, Peg," he said. Then he changed his mind and begged me to stay. He wept; I wavered. His tears turned to angry shouts and blame.

This time I stood my ground: I was going.

Legally, though, I was still married, but separated. It was an uncomfortable situation, setting me apart from almost everyone at Cornell, or perhaps anywhere, and I would keep it a secret. I abandoned the name I'd been using, Peggy Chapman, and signed up for my classes as Margaret Bourke White. That step gave me back my identity, something vitally important that I had been in danger of losing during my years with Chappie.

I had to scramble for money. The Mungers still provided a small stipend, but they assumed that as a married woman with a professor husband I didn't need as much help, and I didn't tell them that my status had changed. In exchange for meals I worked a few hours a day as a waitress in the dining hall, and I took shifts at the front desk in the girls' dormitory to pay for my room.

I was surrounded by natural beauty, Fall Creek carving its way toward Cayuga Lake, the breathtaking falls and gorges sculpted by glaciers. There was the manmade beauty of campus architecture as well: the ornate iron gates of the football stadium, the ivy-covered walls of the stately buildings. I went out with my camera, hiking above the falls for sweeping scenic shots, scouring the campus for the detail that captured the whole, and sometimes combining the two in what I called "campus pattern pictures."

But my coursework took up almost all my time. The solution was to give up waiting tables and eat what I could, when I could. Food had never been important to me, but taking pictures was the one thing I realized I cared about intensely.

I was still influenced by Clarence White's theory that every photograph must be a work of art, like a painting. It wasn't only a matter of finding the correct angle, waiting for the perfect circumstances, and then having the light exactly right. I still aimed for a soft focus, stretching a silk stocking over the lens or manipulating the film in the darkroom using sheets of celluloid to achieve the dreamy effect I wanted. I thought of my pictures as "Pseudo-Corots," referring to the French painter Camille Corot, known for his atmospheric landscapes.

I printed up enlargements of eight or ten I thought were good enough and took them to the campus housing manager, Mr. Coleman, who had found me my jobs as a waitress and a receptionist. I laid the photographs on his desk, one at a time. "Do you think I could sell these?" I asked.

Mr. Coleman adjusted his spectacles and whistled softly. "I'm sure you can."

Working furiously over the Thanksgiving holiday, I matted the photographs and arranged them on easels outside my dormitory dining room. The "Pseudo-Corots" were an immediate success. Girls loved them and wanted to buy them as Christmas gifts for their parents. Mr. Coleman helped recruit twenty students as salesmen to make the rounds of fraternity and sorority houses. Orders poured in.

When Mr. Coleman learned that I'd been developing film in washtubs in the laundry room, he gave me the key to the darkroom in the student supply store. I spent what little money I had and borrowed more to buy chemicals and printing paper. It was almost impossible to keep up. I worked hour after hour every night before I went off to classes in the morning, completely exhausted but also exhilarated.

Mr. Coleman's boss found out that I'd been in the darkroom all night. "You're going to get sick," he worried, "or flunk out, or both, and I don't want it on my hands. I can't allow you to use the darkroom anymore."

I pleaded, but it was useless. Mr. Coleman agreed with his boss, but he gave me the name of a commercial photographer in downtown Ithaca. "Go talk to Henry Head. He'll have good advice."

I took a batch of my photographs to Mr. Head, who reluctantly agreed to look at them. When he'd finished flipping through them, he said, "You can use the darkroom as much as you want, and pay me a percentage of every picture you sell." Sales went well, and I often worked in Mr. Head's darkroom through the night.

When I wasn't shut up in the darkroom, I was out taking pictures around the campus. One night after a heavy snowfall I wanted to photograph the Hall of Science before anyone else's footprints could spoil the image. I carefully walked a long, curving trail through the snow that would accent the stark angles of the building.

After the fiasco at Purdue with the ruined sorority pictures, my confidence had returned. During the two years with Chappie, I'd kept a diary, but there were many days when I left the pages blank, rather than fill them with my unhappiness. Now I wrote about the pictures I was taking, and how I felt. "I know that I'm good and getting better," I wrote. "I know that I am destined for the kind of greatness that famous photographers like Alfred Stieglitz have achieved and very few women have. I'm absolutely certain that I will be among them."

But I was not the best businesswoman. I had not calculated that the rush to buy the photographs as Christmas gifts would end suddenly, and I had unwisely spent all my cash on a pile of photographic paper I didn't need and probably wouldn't need for quite a while. That was a hard lesson. The mistake cost me dearly, and I vowed I would not make it again.

17

Final Break—1927

I DID NOT GO TO CLEVELAND TO SPEND CHRISTMAS
with my mother and Roger. If I wanted to graduate in June, I
had to study through the holidays to rescue my sinking grades.
The train cost too much. But the real reason was I didn't want to
be in the same city as Chappie. It would have been too painful.
Although I didn't love him the way I once did, he represented the
greatest failure of my life, my marriage. I stayed on the deserted
campus over the holidays.

Mr. Head and his wife invited me to come to their house on
New Year's Day for their traditional pork and sauerkraut dinner.
It was kind of them, but I excused myself before the coffee was
served. "The light is perfect for photographing Triphammer Falls,
and I can't bear to miss that opportunity," I explained.

I didn't want to offend Mrs. Head, but I knew that Mr. Head
understood perfectly.

My exams went fairly well, and my grades were satisfactory if
not stellar. In my final semester I signed up for a journalism course.
Other students in the class were hoping to become newspaper
reporters; I was more interested in magazine work and submitted

a photo-essay—pictures of doorways with very little text—for an assignment. The professor was the advisor for the *Cornell Alumni News*, and he thought the editor might want to feature my photographs of campus buildings. The editor looked them over and paid me five dollars each for three pictures. It seemed like a fortune! When the magazine came out, several graduates of the department of architecture wrote to praise the pictures, and one alumnus suggested that I specialize in architectural photography. He said my pictures were that good. It was the encouragement I craved.

But I wasn't sure that with no professional experience I could actually land such a job—and I did need to find work. To play it safe, I sent an application to the American Museum of Natural History in New York. The curator of herpetology invited me to come for an interview. He seemed so impressed by my application that I thought the offer of a position might be imminent.

I was nearly twenty-two, about to graduate, and unsure which to follow—my head and my long interest in natural science, or my heart and my passion for photography. A job at the museum would be the safe choice. Or I could try to pursue a career in architectural photography, even though I had no specific training in the field. I had to know if the men who praised my photographs were right, or if they simply enjoyed my pictures of their alma mater. My future hung in the balance.

I asked the letter-writer to recommend someone qualified to give me an objective opinion. His reply: "See Benjamin Moskowitz, York & Sawyer, Architects, NYC. Good luck."

During the Easter vacation I booked a cheap room and took the train to New York City, where I arrived late on Thursday and went straight to the Park Avenue address of York & Sawyer. At their office on the twenty-third floor I asked the switchboard operator for Mr. Moskowitz.

"I think Mr. Moskowitz has already left, miss. I know he was planning a long weekend. Did you have an appointment?"

I hadn't counted on this. I shook my head. "But I've come all this way! And I can't stay until next week to see him! I have to be back on campus for classes!"

She sighed and asked my name and told me to wait while she tried to see if he might still be there. I paced nervously, thinking that my time and money and my best chance for an expert opinion had been thrown away. The operator rang his office; no answer. "Sorry, but it looks like you're out of luck, Miss White," she said.

Why hadn't I planned this better? Called for an appointment? Taken an earlier train? How could I have made such a mistake? I was close to tears.

Just then a tall, gray-haired man, beautifully groomed, strode through the reception area. The switchboard operator signaled me and mouthed, "That's him."

I didn't hesitate. "Oh, Mr. Moskowitz!" I called out. "Just a moment, sir, please! I'd like to speak to you."

He glanced at his expensive-looking gold watch and kept walking. "Sorry, I have a train to catch," he said brusquely. "I don't believe you had an appointment."

I hurried after him toward the elevator. "I apologize, sir, but I was told to talk to you and to show you some photographs." I mentioned the Cornell graduate who had given me his name.

He pressed the button to call the elevator. "As I said, Miss—?"

"Margaret Bourke White."

"Miss White, I have a train to catch. I'm sure your photographs are very good or he would not have sent you to see me, but unfortunately I have no time to look at them or talk to you now."

He checked his watch impatiently and rang again for the elevator. "It's always slow when I'm most in a hurry," he muttered.

"Let me show you just one photograph while we're waiting," I pleaded, and opened the portfolio. The picture on top was a view of the river from the library tower, the highest point on campus. I'd climbed that tower at dawn and at sunset and at every possible time in between to catch the light on the water at exactly the right moment and framed the shot through lacy grillwork.

Mr. Moskowitz glanced at it, impatiently at first and then more carefully a second time. "You took this photograph?" he asked doubtfully.

"Yes, these pictures are all my work." I rushed through my story—the elevator could arrive at any moment. "Mr. Moskowitz, I have to know if you think I have the ability to become a professional in this field."

The elevator gate clattered open. "Going down!"

"Never mind, Chester," Mr. Moskowitz told the operator. "We don't need you now." He motioned for me to follow him. "Come with me. I want to have a look at the rest of these."

As we hurried through the reception room, Mr. Moskowitz called out to the switchboard operator, "Ring up Sawyer and York and anyone else who's still here and tell them to come to the conference room."

The windows of the walnut-paneled room looked out over Park Avenue, but the men in pinstriped suits and silk neckties weren't interested in that view. They were gazing at my photographs, propped on a narrow ledge along the walls. They liked what they saw.

For the next hour they asked me questions about my age—I fibbed a bit, adding a couple of years—my education, and my experience. At the end of the hour I walked out of the offices of York & Sawyer with their assurance that any architect in the country would willingly pay for my services. I wanted to celebrate, and when I stopped for something to eat, I could scarcely keep from telling my good news to the tired-looking waitress behind the counter.

The next day I visited the Museum of Natural History because I was interested in the exhibits, but not because I wanted to work there. I left a note for the curator, explaining that I was unable to make my appointment. I knew it was a risk; I needed a job, and the museum probably would have offered me one in herpetology. But I wanted a different kind of life.

For hours I wandered the broad avenues and narrow side streets of New York. I gazed up at skyscrapers, seeing dozens of potential shots and wishing I had my camera. I stopped in an elegant stationery shop and bought a leather-bound notebook and a pricey silver fountain pen for jotting down ideas. I imagined myself living in the city. But although the architects at York & Sawyer had praised my work and declared that it was of professional quality, they had not offered me a position. I would be my own employer with no regular paycheck, always worried about money. It was surely the way nearly all artists lived, and that was a scary thought.

As the train followed the Hudson River north, I took out my notebook and pen and tried to imagine the shape a new life might take. I needed to come up with a concrete plan.

◆◆

As spring began to emerge in Ithaca, I kept taking pictures. I still didn't fit in, but that didn't bother me. There was no man in my life; my camera was everything. I was lonely at times, but I endured it. Loneliness was not as bad as being with someone who didn't love me enough.

In May a letter arrived, postmarked Cleveland, addressed in Chappie's handwriting. I propped it unopened on my dresser. After two days I tore open the envelope and read the letter.

He wrote that he was doing well at Lincoln Electric,

specializing in electric welding, and he was in line for a promotion. He missed me and thought of me often. He regretted the pain he had caused me and believed he had become more mature.

"We are still man and wife," he wrote. "And my fondest hope is that we can still find our way back to the deep love we once shared. I propose to come to Ithaca so that we may talk face to face. I long to see you. Please write and let me know how you feel." He signed it, "All my love, Chappie."

Everything that had been so clear to me now seemed confused. *All my love?* What about his mother? Chappie had not stood up to the Duchess of Detroit when I needed him to. Would he stand up for me now? I doubted it. And what about those black silences when I left the apartment a mess because I'd been out taking photographs?

But I was anxious to hear what he had to say, to untangle my feelings. We had once been deeply in love. Maybe there was still something we could salvage.

I wrote back and said, "Yes, come."

I went to the depot to meet his train, got there too early, and waited nervously. The first sight of him stepping off the train, handsome as ever with the same brilliant smile, sent a jolt of excitement through me, and I resisted the urge to run toward him and throw myself into his arms. He set down his suitcase. Neither of us made a move to embrace. We stood there, as awkward as a first date.

"You've cut your hair," he said.

"Yes," I said. "How was the trip?"

"Fine, fine. You look good, Peggy. Ithaca apparently agrees with you."

"Thank you. Yes, I suppose it does."

It was not far to the hotel where I'd booked him a room. While we walked there, he told me that his ancient Dodge had finally called it quits. Now we had something that was easy to talk about: the auto's last days, the bicycle he used to get to work, his plans to buy another automobile. "I'm thinking of the Model T Ford, but Momma thinks I should wait until I've saved up more money."

There she was: Momma.

"And what are you planning to do?" I asked, already guessing the answer.

Chappie shrugged. "She's probably right. I promised to help her and Poppa before I buy something for myself."

The most important questions had now been answered. Everything was as it had always been—that was the painful truth.

The hotel lunchroom where we stopped for something to eat was not a place where students usually came, but I recognized a girl from my journalism class at a nearby table. She looked at Chappie and raised her eyebrows, probably expecting me to introduce him. She had no idea who he was—*my husband*—and I had no intention of revealing that part of my life to anyone here. I smiled and waved.

After lunch we went for a long walk, and I showed him the falls and pointed out the buildings I had photographed. I considered telling him about my trip to New York, but didn't. I thought about showing him my portfolio of architectural photographs, but didn't do that either. Chappie's questions weren't about my pictures— they were about my science courses. What were my plans? Had I had any job interviews? I shook my head and didn't mention the interview I could have had in New York or my conversation with the architects.

At dinner that evening I asked about his work. He was involved in developing the kind of steel that would be used in building streamlined trains, and he was excited about that.

His other news was that he'd gotten a cat.

We lingered over coffee. The other diners had left the restaurant; the waiters were clearing everything away, making it plain that it was closing time. Chappie reached across the table and took my hand. "Will you come up to my room with me, Peg?" he asked.

"I'd rather not," I said. "But we can go back to the lobby in my residence hall, if you'd like to talk."

"We're still married," he said. "I still love you. I believe we could work it out, if you're willing. I came here to ask you to come back to Cleveland. Let's try again. Please."

I looked into the dark eyes of the man I'd once loved and promised to love until death parted us. But Chappie had hurt me deeply, less by what he had done than by what he had not done. I saw no possibility of finding that love again.

"No," I said. "I will be your friend, but I will not be your wife."

He stayed in Ithaca only two days. There wasn't much else to talk about. I didn't see him off at the train, saying I had other commitments, which was the truth. I felt very little now for Chappie, except regret. I was like an automobile with no reverse gear; I could only go forward, even if I didn't know where that would take me.

◆◆

Visitors were flocking to campus for commencement exercises, and I arranged for the sale of those stacks of prints left over from the previous winter. I recruited a couple of students to help me set up displays in the library and the dining halls; others made the rounds of fraternities and sororities. Before commencement weekend was over, my entire stock was sold out, and I had made a nice profit.

And I also had a plan. I loved the idea of New York, but I believed the city was so competitive, so hard to make a living in, that I would end up taking on too much monotonous work to pay the rent. How would I ever grow as a photographer, if I was always scrambling to survive? Maybe someday I could live in New York, but not yet.

I would move back to Cleveland. The first step was to write to Mr. Moskowitz and ask him for the names of Cleveland architects who had graduated from Cornell. This was the city where I could launch my career as an architectural photographer.

Cleveland—1927

I PACKED UP MY DIPLOMA AND MY CAMERA, CAUGHT
the train from Ithaca to Buffalo, and boarded the night boat
across Lake Erie to Cleveland. I was on the deck of *The City of
Buffalo* when it sidled up to the pier, paddlewheels churning,
the outlines of Cleveland emerging from the early morning mist.
When I'd lived here three years earlier as Peggy Chapman, I'd
explored the docks and railroads and foundries with the idea of
making a photographic portrait of the city. But my teaching, my
college classes, and my troubled marriage hadn't left me the time
or energy to follow through. Now I was ready for anything.

After a cup of coffee to wake me up, I went to my mother's
house. I found her preparing to rush off to work at the school for
the blind. She seemed happy to see me, but she went directly to
the question looming most important in her mind. "What about
Chappie?"

"That's over," I said. "You were right. We were too young."
There was much more to it, but it was still too painful to talk about.
I wondered if I'd ever be able to tell her about Mrs. Chapman's
cruel words or Chappie's black moods.

She looked at me for a long moment and sighed. "I'm truly sorry, Margaret," she said. "I so much wanted this to be the right thing for you. I'm sure you didn't choose the easy way." Then she straightened up and said briskly, "The little room is ready for you. I don't mind telling you, it will be nice to have you home again. It's been awfully lonely since your father died. And I know Roger will be glad to have you around."

I didn't have the heart to tell her then that I wanted to be on my own, and not have to answer questions or offer explanations when my camera kept me out until all hours.

Almost on cue, my sixteen-year-old brother stumbled into the kitchen, rumpled and yawning. I had not seen much of Roger over the past few years, and he appeared to have changed from a timid little boy into a great, hulking young male. "Hi, Peg."

Mother frowned, her mood making a right-angle turn from pleasure at seeing me again to disapproval at this monosyllabic creature now denuding the icebox.

"Would you care for some breakfast, Margaret?" Mother asked, adding pointedly, "I assume there's a little something left. But you'll have to fix it yourself. I must leave for work."

As soon as Mother was out the door, Roger visibly relaxed. He dropped a blob of butter into the frying pan. "Want some eggs? Scrambled or fried?"

"Over easy."

Roger cracked two eggs into the sizzling butter. "You are so damn lucky, Peg," he said. Had he actually said *damn*? "You remember how she grilled me when I was a little kid? And I had to tell her everything that happened? Even my dreams! I used to make things up, just to get her off my back. And it's no better since Father died. Worse, in fact." He flipped the eggs expertly, turned them out onto a plate, and sat down across from me.

"I didn't realize it was so hard for you," I said. "Mother didn't question me about my dreams, but she was very demanding. 'Always take the harder path,' she told me. She wanted us to be successful, and she knew it wasn't going to be easy."

"I just wish she'd get married again," Roger said, finishing one glass of milk and pouring another.

"You say that, but you'd change your tune if she did. Marriage isn't the cure for anything. I promise you that."

Roger looked at me closely. "You and Chappie are done for?"

My throat tightened, and I felt tears welling. My reaction caught me off guard. I'd thought I was over Chappie. "Yes," I whispered.

"Sorry," Roger mumbled. "Shouldn't have asked. None of my business."

"Let's talk about *you*. What are your plans?"

He grimaced. "Finish school and get the hell out of here."

"Worthy goals," I said. "Nothing beyond that?"

He shook his head. "Not yet," he growled. He collected his books and headed out the door.

"Thanks for breakfast," I called after him, then carried my dishes to the sink and washed them and my brother's—better than I would have done when Chappie and I were together.

I unpacked a few things and planned my next moves. Mr. Moskowitz had sent the list of architects I'd asked for. I would start calling on them right away. I didn't expect it to be easy. I was young, only twenty-three, and that might equal "inexperienced" in the eyes of some. More of a problem than my age—I could always fib about that—was my gender. Few women were architects, few were photographers, and if any were architectural photographers, I hadn't heard of them.

I knew that I had to sell myself before I could sell my photographs, and to do that, I had to look as though I knew exactly what I was doing. First, I needed a professional-looking outfit. The Mungers had sent a generous graduation check, and I used it to go shopping. I invested in a smartly tailored gray suit, two plain white blouses, one blue hat and matching gloves, one red hat and matching gloves, and a pair of sturdy black pumps.

Dressed in one of my outfits, I left my mother's house in Cleveland Heights the next day, rode the streetcar into the city, and pounded the sidewalks with my photographs. I went from one architect's office to the next along Euclid Avenue, Cleveland's main boulevard. The trick was to talk my way past the receptionist, flashing a bright smile. Sometimes I met a minor associate and offered to show my portfolio. Sometimes I got an appointment to come back. More often I was greeted with a flat "No thanks, we don't need your services." I did this day after day.

When the offices closed for the lunch hour, I stopped for a cream cheese sandwich in a diner or a hot dog from a cart on the street. At the end of the day, exhausted and feeling I could not smile and chat my way into one more office, I visited the shoeshine parlor on lower Euclid, where a little old Italian shoemaker cleaned and polished my pumps. While I waited, my stocking feet on a sheet of newspaper, I made notes on file cards, one for each firm I'd called on, with information about whom I'd met and what had been said, and whether I'd worn the red hat and gloves or the blue ones. Then I caught the streetcar back to my mother's house, ate supper with Mother and Roger, and indulged in a long, hot bath.

Weeks passed. There were a few vague promises: "We can't give you anything now, Miss White, but come back and see us in a month or so." But no assignments. It was hard not to get discouraged.

One rainy morning in September I slipped into the courthouse I passed nearly every day and filed the papers for my divorce, writing the final chapter of my marriage. I added a hyphen to my name: Margaret Bourke-White. With a hyphenated name people were less likely to call me "Margaret White," and I thought it sounded more professional.

I had promised myself that I would move out of my mother's house and into a place of my own when I was paid for my first assignment. I didn't have an assignment yet, but after I filed for a divorce, I felt a new sense of my independence. I withdrew all of my savings and rented a minuscule apartment in a slightly seedy part of Cleveland between downtown, with its tall office buildings, and the Cuyahoga River. It was drably furnished with a stained rug and a lumpy couch plus a few mismatched dishes. There was a sink in the tiny kitchen where I could develop my films and a rust-stained bathtub where I could rinse them. That was all I needed. I called it the Bourke-White Studio and ordered letterhead and business cards.

The first time Mother saw my studio, she shook her head and said, "Well, I suppose it's a beginning."

Finally I got my first commission.

A wealthy woman contacted me; a landscape architect I'd called on had suggested that I might be the person to photograph her rose garden. This wasn't the kind of commission I wanted, but I was in no position to turn it down. The light was perfect, the roses were at their peak, and the shoot went extraordinarily well. I had taped black cloth over the two windows for a makeshift darkroom, but light nevertheless leaked in while I was developing the film and fogged the negatives. I was sick, but determined—there was still a chance to get it right.

When I rushed back to the garden the next morning, the sun shone brightly, but a rainstorm had swept through during the night. Petals from the rosebushes littered the ground. There was no way to recover from this mistake. It was like a repeat of the sorority pictures I'd ruined in Indiana. Again I had failed miserably, and for the first time since I'd returned to Cleveland, I sat down and cried.

I pressed on, showing my portfolio and leaving my card, over and over. Then one day, wearing my red gloves and red hat—I had worn blue the first time—I made a follow-up visit to the offices of Pitkin and Mott. They were young, only a few years older than I was, and they had not been in business long. Mr. Mott sported an impressive mustache but was not yet successful enough to have gold cufflinks. On my first visit he'd told me that *Architecture* magazine wanted to do a feature on a school he and Mr. Pitkin had designed, if they could provide good pictures of the finished building. The job had been assigned to another photographer, but his pictures hadn't met the standards of the magazine's editor.

"Perhaps you can do better," said Mr. Mott. "We'll pay you five dollars a picture if your work is satisfactory."

He gave me the address of the school, and I went to look it over. The building was handsome, but it sat amid a sea of mud, surrounded by piles of leftover lumber, pipes, and roofing. Mountains of dirt had been dug out for the foundation and trash was left everywhere by workmen. I studied the building from every angle, thinking which might work best. Sunsets always yield a flattering light, so that was when I would return with my camera.

The next few days were rainy or cloudy. When the weather finally cleared, I discovered that the sun wasn't setting where I thought it would and was brilliantly illuminating the wrong side of the building. Sunrise would have to do. For the next four days I arrived at the site before dawn, but the sun came up through a thick haze that didn't burn off quickly enough. On the fifth morning, conditions were perfect, but now I saw a new problem: the rising sun illuminated not only the best angles of the school but all the trash around it.

Off I hurried to find a flower shop, coaxed the proprietor

144

to open early, and begged him to sell me whatever flowers were cheapest that day. The best price was on asters, and I splurged on as many as I could carry. I lugged them back to the schoolyard and stuck them in the ground in the foreground of the first shot I planned to make. Squatting in the mud, I aimed my camera so that the flowers blotted out the ugly surroundings. Then I pulled up the asters and transplanted them to the next location. If you believed the photographs, the handsome schoolhouse existed in the midst of a lovely autumn garden. Fortunately I had worn an old dress and sweater and a neglected pair of cotton stockings, because I was a mud-covered mess by the time I'd finished.

The next day I returned to the offices of Pitkin and Mott with a dozen fine photographs. Mott's mustache twitched with amusement and pleasure at the instant landscaping I'd created, and they bought the whole dozen. "I know the magazine will accept these," said Mott. "And we'll all benefit when they're published," Pitkin chimed in.

But publication was months away, and the sixty dollars I collected would have been spent by then. I continued to make the rounds in search of work that paid, leaving little time to take the kind of photographs that I loved.

One day as I was carrying my portfolio to call on yet another prospect, I passed through a large open space known as Public Square. A Negro preacher stood on a soapbox, delivering an impassioned sermon to a square that was deserted except for a flock of pigeons that ignored him. Preacher and pigeons would have made a wonderful photograph, if I'd had a camera. But my camera was back in my apartment.

I'd passed a camera store many times on my way to the shoeshine parlor, and I raced down the street to find it. The short, middle-aged man in thick eyeglasses behind the counter goggled as I burst in, shouting, "I need a camera right away! Do you have one I can borrow? Or rent? There's a perfect photograph out there begging to be taken!" I waved in the direction of the preacher and the pigeons.

The man behind the counter hauled a Graflex down from a shelf and handed it over without stopping to ask for a deposit, my name, or any sort of identification. I rushed out with the camera, heading for the hotdog cart to buy a bag of peanuts, and sprinted back to Public Square.

The preacher was still there, still ranting, but now the pigeons had left. Several young boys were hanging around a street corner, and for a few pennies apiece I hired them. "Go scatter these nuts in front of the preacher," I instructed. The boys stared at me, shrugged, and then did as I told them. The pigeons flocked back, the preacher now had an audience, and I had the photograph I wanted.

The story ended even better than I could have hoped: the man who had loaned me the camera suggested I show the picture of the preacher to the Cleveland Chamber of Commerce, which paid ten dollars for it and put it on the cover of their monthly magazine.

My benefactor's name was Alfred Bemis. He'd spent all his life around cameras and darkrooms, and he became my teacher and mentor. I called him Beme.

19

MY PHOTOGRAPHIC STYLE WAS CHANGING. I MOVED away from the soft focus Clarence White advocated and dis-covered the raw beauty in the swampy, gritty area of Cleveland known as the Flats.

The Flats began where the tall, dignified office buildings ended. The Cuyahoga River slashed the Flats in two. Bridges with trestles resembling abstract sculptures spanned it; railroad tracks chopped it crosswise. Great arches that would soon support more railroad tracks reached across the sky and stitched the parts together. Tugboats nudged barges down the river toward Lake Erie, locomotives hauled cars back and forth, and towering smokestacks shot sparks toward the sky. There were mills and factories everywhere. With my camera I could capture the clamor and confusion of a factory in a way that words could not.

On the day I borrowed the camera, Beme said when I returned it, "Let's go have lunch. You look as though you could use something to eat." Between mouthfuls of ham on rye, I told him how my love for factories and steel mills had started when I was a little girl and my father took me to the foundry.

"I've never forgotten it," I said. "I can still picture that fiery cascade of liquid metal and the shower of sparks just as vividly as if it were yesterday. It has inspired what I want to do now."

"Yes," he said. "I see that. But you have some mustard on your chin."

Beme did everything possible to teach me and everything imaginable to help me. "You should have your own enlarger," he said when he'd seen what I was using, and somehow he found the parts to cobble one together for me. "You've got to have more than one camera," he said. "I know you love your Ica, but you don't use the same camera for a portrait that you do for a landscape or the close-up of a piece of machinery. You should have at least two more. Three or four would be best."

"Beme, you know I can't afford that!"

"Never mind. Eventually you will."

Beme knew that I worried about what other photographers were doing—Edward Weston, who could make a woman's knees look like a piece of sculpture; Alfred Stieglitz and his clouds; Paul Strand's geometric compositions. But Beme banished my anxiety with one piece of advice I never forgot: "Go ahead, little girl. Never mind what anybody else is doing. Shoot off your own cannon."

He hovered over me like a worried nanny. "You're too thin," he dithered. "You're not eating right, are you? And you've got dark circles under your eyes. Do you ever get a decent night's sleep?" He knew the answer to both questions; I often neglected to eat, and I spent too many nights developing photographs, the only times my apartment was truly a darkroom.

Beme introduced me to Earl Leiter, a photofinisher who developed photographic film and made prints from the negatives. Earl occupied the darkroom on the fifth floor above the camera shop, and he possessed all the technical expertise that I was lacking. I had an unerring eye for a great subject when I saw it, and my instinct for setting up the shot was excellent. But I made too many mistakes in the darkroom. Chappie once told me, "You have the best eye, but I know how to get the best pictures out of the exposed film." Earl was like that, too.

When I worried about my darkroom skills, Beme reassured me, "You can make a technician, and there are a million of them out there, but you can't make a photographer. I can teach you some techniques, but the rest is up to you."

I still rotated the red-hat-and-gloves set with the blue as accessories to my plain gray suit and prim white blouse, but because I was calling on the same companies so often, I needed another outfit. I used my mother's sewing machine to make myself a purple dress and stitched up a set of camera cloths to cover my head when I was focusing my camera on a tripod—a blue cloth for the blue hat and gloves, a black one to go with the red, and purple to match my new dress.

"I worry about you, Margaret," my mother remarked as I pumped the treadle of the sewing machine. "Are you earning enough to make ends meet?"

"Somehow it always works out," I said above the chatter of the machine. "If I overdraw my bank account by a few dollars in the morning, by the end of the day I always manage to sell a couple of prints to cover it. And the Chamber of Commerce just ordered several more photographs, so I'm in good shape for a while." I bit off a thread. "My goal is to sell enough pictures so I can make the kind of pictures that fascinate me."

She threw up her hands. "Living hand-to-mouth, that's what it is! I just hope you're better at handling money than your father was."

It was late fall in Ohio, and the clouds were spectacular, glowing as though they were lit from within by thousands of candles. Every spare hour during the week and all day Sunday, I spent taking pictures in the Flats. Once, when I was alone around eleven o'clock at night, I was accosted by two policemen.

"Whatcha think yer doin' out here at this hour, young lady?" demanded the younger, taller cop.

"Why, I'm taking pictures!" I explained with a big smile. "Just look at how that bridge gleams in the moonlight! Have you ever seen anything like it? And over there"—I pointed to flame-colored smoke erupting from a tall stack—"won't that be a great shot?"

"By golly, she's right," growled the older, paunchy cop. "But it's dangerous for you to be here alone, miss. Some men might get the wrong idea and mistake you for a lady of the evening. Let us tag along, to make sure you're safe."

I thanked them, and they stayed with me until I was done and promised to watch out for me whenever they were assigned that beat.

Finally, I got a real break. I heard that the public relations officer for Union Trust Bank was looking for a photograph to use on the cover of their monthly magazine. I showed him my portfolio. He flipped through it, stopping at a photograph I'd done of the new High Level Bridge, which soared above the Cuyahoga River. "This one," he said. "Fifty dollars."

It would have been unprofessional to jump up and down and clap my hands, so I simply nodded and said, "An excellent choice."

Each month I went back to the bank and sold another picture—of bridges, trains, smokestacks, factories, steel mills, the whole industrial landscape of the Flats. No one told me what to photograph. They liked my work and gave me a free hand. Now I had an almost guaranteed income of fifty dollars a month!

I also earned money working for wealthy people, taking pictures of their beautiful mansions and carefully tended gardens, manicured lawns, and shimmering reflecting pools. I delivered the finished photographs in a handsome custom package that looked expensive, and I charged high prices to make sure my clients appreciated the work they were getting.

But my fanatical dedication to my work left no time for a social life, and I had few friends. My brother, Roger, busy with who knows what, was rarely around when I visited Mother. Ruth was working in Chicago. Mostly I was alone, except for Beme, who was like a doting uncle, and brotherly Earl, and I was happier than I had ever been in my life. I bought a battered old green Chevy, named it Patrick, and enjoyed a new kind of freedom. My twin goals—to be a famous photographer and a rich one—were beginning to feel like real possibilities, not just idle pipe dreams, and my drive to reach them kept me focused.

◆ ◆

The year 1927 was an exciting time to be in Cleveland. A new skyscraper was going up on Public Square—Terminal Tower, with fifty-two floors, designed to be one of the tallest buildings in the world. Two mysterious brothers, the Van Sweringens, known around Cleveland as "the Vans," were financing the project. They had the power to buy up almost anything they wanted, especially railroads, and the money to build whatever they chose. Rumors circulated that they planned to have their private apartments at the very top, accessible by a secret elevator.

I photographed the Vans' tower at all times of the day and night from a distance as it climbed higher. I longed to get closer to it, and one day I decided to simply ignore the fences and barriers and KEEP OUT signs, skirted around them, and set up my camera.

In less than a minute I heard a watchman shouting at me. I pretended not to hear him until his hand clamped down hard on my shoulder. "Just what in blazes do you think you're doing?" he roared.

"Just trying to take a picture, sir," I said, smiling apologetically.

He ordered me away, telling me not to come back under any circumstances, and I had to obey. I vowed that someday I would have my studio in Terminal Tower, but first I had to establish my reputation, and that was taking longer than I wanted. Something big had to happen.

20

A New Direction—1927

MY FRIENDS AT UNION TRUST CALLED TO ASK ME TO photograph a prize steer in the bank lobby. No explanation of how it got there, or why.

I paid a call on my subject, a jet-black devil with fearsome horns, a fierce eye, and a belligerent reaction to finding himself in a roped-off enclosure surrounded by stark white marble. A couple of schoolboys had raised the steer for a school project, and the photographs would be used as part of the bank's public relations program.

I ran to Beme for help. When I described the black subject and the glaring white background, Beme figured out that I would have to use artificial light. I'd never used flash powder. Beme promised to lend me what I needed and, in the interests of safety to myself and anyone who happened to be in the lobby as well as the steer, he would also lend me Earl Leiter.

The beast was snorting and stomping and tossing his massive head when Earl showed up. Earl and I climbed gingerly over the ropes and began to set up our equipment. A curious crowd gathered to watch, as though we were a pair of matadors at a bullfight. The steer bellowed.

"Timing is everything," Earl said. "I'll set off the flash powder just as you trip the shutter."

I put my head under the blue camera cloth. The steer lowered his head, swished his tail, and glared straight into my lens. I froze.

"What's wrong?" Earl muttered.

"I can't remember how to do this," I whimpered. "Beme told me exactly what to do, and now I've forgotten everything he said."

Earl's hand reached surreptitiously beneath the camera cloth and fumbled for the shutter release cable. "Focused?" he whispered.

"Focused," I breathed from under the cloth.

Earl set off the charges of flash powder, simultaneously clicking the shutter. There was a burst of light and a billow of smoke. A cloud of ashes rained down. The steer appeared stunned. Earl and I grabbed our gear, climbed over the ropes, and raced back to Earl's darkroom. A short time later I returned with a proof of the photo to show to the bank officials. It was not my greatest photograph, but it did portray a powerful beast pawing the ground and poised for a charge.

The bankers were pleased. They wanted 485 copies by the next morning to distribute to newspapers and schools. "Can you do that, Miss Bourke-White?"

"Certainly," I said, wondering if I actually could do it, and rushed to tell Earl and Beme the news.

"Four hundred and eighty-five glossy prints?" Beme groaned, slapping his forehead. "You're kidding, right? You couldn't print that many in a week with that enlarger of yours, even if you worked around the clock."

"Maybe some commercial studio could do it," I suggested, worried that I was about to lose everything.

"Not a chance, kiddo. Not a chance."

I blinked back tears. Beme grimaced. "Okay, okay, cheer up. We'll give it our best shot."

After the camera shop closed for the day, with me behind Patrick's wheel, Beme beside me, and Earl wedged in the back seat, we drove to a steakhouse to fortify ourselves for a long night. Then we climbed up to Earl's fifth-floor darkroom and went to work. Around one o'clock, with almost half the order left to go, we ran out of the ferrotype tins used to put a glossy finish on photographs. Beme rounded up all the tins he had in stock.

"Never fear, kiddo," Beme said, "I'll wrap 'em all up just like new when we're done, and nobody will ever be the wiser."

We finished sometime around dawn. I knew very well that I couldn't have pulled this off without Beme and Earl. I still had a lot to learn. Beme promised to have the prints delivered to the bank. "Go get some sleep. You look like you're about to pass out."

Bleary-eyed, I took the long way home, driving past the steel mills just as the sun was coming up. On a high point overlooking the Otis Steel plant, I pulled over and watched a line of slag cars filled with the waste remaining after the metal had been separated from the ore. One by one the cars dumped the red-hot slag in a brilliant cascade down the hillside.

The sight re-ignited my desire to get inside a steel mill; the question was how to accomplish that. I'd tried several times, but each time I asked, I was told the same story about a visiting schoolteacher who had keeled over in a dead faint from the heat and the fumes. It had happened some twenty years earlier, but the story was repeated as though it was a biblical truth. The message was that women were not welcome.

A few days later, when Beme and I were eating goulash in a restaurant near the camera shop, I asked, "So how do I wangle my way into a mill? That fainting schoolteacher has made it impossible."

"It all comes down to who you know," Beme said. "So, kiddo, who do you know who's got connections?"

I made a list of everybody I'd done work for and thought of Mr.

John Sherwin, the president of the bank where I'd photographed the steer. Mrs. Sherwin had once hired me to photograph her garden. When I found out that Mr. Sherwin was on the board of Otis Steel, I called for an appointment. His secretary informed me that he was a *very* busy man, but I persisted until he agreed to see me.

"Stunning photograph of the animal, my dear," said the courtly Mr. Sherwin, "but I cannot understand why a pretty young girl like you, who takes such lovely pictures of gardens and flowers and the like, would want to be around rough-talking workers in a dirty, noisy steel mill." He sighed. "But if you're determined to do this, I'll send a letter to Mr. Kulas. He's the president of Otis."

I told Beme about my triumph, knowing he'd be as excited as I was. But I had something else on my mind: I wanted to ask him for a loan. Beme had often told me, "If you need a few bucks to get you through, just say the word."

I needed more than a few bucks. I needed fifty dollars. To look the part of a successful professional when I walked into Mr. Kulas's office, it would take more than just a hat and matching gloves. I had my eye on a sheared beaver jacket I'd seen in a shop window.

Beme looked at me incredulously. "You can barely pay your rent, and you want to buy a fur coat?"

"It will be a good investment. You have to spend money to make money."

Beme rolled his eyes. Then he pulled out a sheaf of bills and peeled off five tens. I bought the jacket and wore it back to the camera shop to model it.

"You do look swell, I'll grant you that," Beme acknowledged gruffly.

Mr. Sherwin kept his word, and a week later I had an appointment with the president of Otis Steel. Confident in my furs, I marched into Mr. Kulas's office with my portfolio. He occupied a massive leather chair behind a massive mahogany desk and asked me why on earth I wanted to take pictures in a steel mill. He leafed idly through the photographs I'd brought to show him. "Why not stick to flower gardens, which you do so elegantly?"

"Because I see a different kind of beauty in a steel mill, sir," I said.

I had to convince him that I was not trying to sell him anything. I wasn't asking him to buy my pictures. All I wanted was a chance to experiment with a subject that deeply interested me.

"Very well," he said at last, "I will notify the supervisor that you are to be admitted any time you come to the mill. I'm leaving next week for an extended tour of Europe. I hope to see you when I return." He stood up—he was short, stocky, broad-chested, imposing—and reached out to shake my hand. "My best wishes in your endeavors, Miss Bourke-White."

I plunged into my new project. Beme called it my "obsession." He volunteered to go with me that first night, and he looked me over disapprovingly. "What kind of a getup is that? A skirt and high-heeled shoes? You look like you're going to a cocktail party."

I made every mistake possible, not just my clothes. What I wanted to do was beyond me technically. I didn't realize how much I still did not know. I had no idea how to deal with the sharp contrasts of light and shadow. The results were not just disappointing—they were *terrible*.

"Underexposed," Beme pronounced when the film was developed. "There's no actinic value in the light given off by the molten metal."

Actinic value? I didn't know what he was talking about.

"The molten metal gives off a red glow, like the red light you use in the darkroom," he explained. "Red light doesn't register on the negative. You might think it's lighting up the whole place, but it isn't."

Night after night I went back, sometimes alone, sometimes with Earl and Beme. It was a continuing struggle, but it was the most exciting thing I'd ever done. We tried using floodlights and setting off flash powder. We changed lenses and tried different angles, but nothing worked. The mill was too vast, too dark.

At first we had been welcomed into the mill. Then we were tolerated. But now we were a nuisance. My camera and I got in the way. There were places I was absolutely forbidden to go, and I went there anyway, determined to get the kind of artistic shots I could see in my mind's eye, or die trying. And that's what everyone at the mill was afraid would happen—that I'd fall and break my bones or tumble headfirst into a ladle of molten steel.

The night superintendent's attitude ballooned from mild impatience to anger, until he'd had enough. He claimed that I was interfering with the men's regular work. They wanted to help, and they'd drop everything to hold up a shield to keep me from getting burned by the intense heat. I was cutting into their production, he said. Looking out for me was not what they were paid to do. If the boss found out, there would be trouble. The superintendent threw me out.

Even Beme was discouraged. We had exhausted every possibility we could think of to capture the magic of steel-making. It would take a miracle, Beme agreed.

And then a miracle actually did occur. A traveling salesman named Jackson stopped off and visited Beme on his way to Hollywood, where he planned to sell a new type of magnesium flare to the movie industry. Beme thought these big flares might provide the right kind of light for my pictures and talked Jackson into coming to the mill with us one cold, snowy night. We knew when the superintendent took his break, and we could sneak in and evade him long enough to try out Jackson's flares. He agreed to let us use two of them.

Two weren't enough. We tried again, using four. Finally, with only one flare left, I captured a trail of sparks that showed up brilliantly on the negative. Success!

I hugged Jackson. But I'd celebrated too soon.

The negative was perfect, but the prints turned out gray and dull, the fault of the printing paper. I chalked up another failure.

And then a second miracle: a second traveling salesman appeared, this one named Charlie, whose specialty was photographic paper. Over a steak dinner Charlie told us about a new kind of paper that he thought was better suited to the kind of high-contrast dark-and-light photographs I was taking. We left our dinners unfinished and hurried back to the darkroom. The image appeared vividly on this new paper, and the results were exactly what I'd been struggling to achieve. I let out a whoop of pure joy.

I heard that Mr. Kulas was back from Europe. I chose a dozen prints from the many pictures I'd taken inside the mill and mounted them on heavy white stock. I begged Beme to drive to Otis Steel with me. Beme saw how nervous I was and squeezed my hand as I climbed out of the car. "You'll do just fine, kiddo. Nobody's done anything like the pictures you've got in that portfolio."

I headed for the office building, my heels tap-tap-tapping on the wooden trestle across the mill yard and echoing the thudding of my heart. Mr. Kulas was in a meeting, and I had to endure an endless wait until I was finally in front of his desk, clutching my portfolio to keep my hands from shaking.

"Ah, my dear Miss Bourke-White! Here you are! Let me see what you've got."

I watched as he lifted out each print and laid it on his desk until all twelve were lined up perfectly. He studied each one briefly, but his gaze lingered over the photograph of white-hot molten slag overflowing from a ladle and reflecting on the shields that covered the men's faces.

"Amazing," he said. "Absolutely amazing. I'm quite sure no pictures like these have ever been taken before. I'm not even sure anyone has even tried. This is pioneering work. What is your price?"

I allowed myself to breathe. I had told Mr. Kulas the first time we met that I wasn't trying to sell him anything. All I'd asked for was the chance to take photographs. But I knew that wealthy people—and Mr. Kulas was very rich—valued work only if they had to pay handsomely for it. I replied carefully, "You may choose to buy as many or as few as you wish, but the price is one hundred dollars a picture."

"Agreed," he answered shortly and proceeded to pick eight. Then he commissioned me to make another eight. "Our stockholders would be delighted to see these photographs. Corporate clients, too. Perhaps in a book—*The Story of Steel*, or some such. Privately printed, expensively done, fine stock, nicely bound, everything first class. Eh, Miss Bourke-White? What do you think?"

I was nearly speechless, thinking of the eight hundred dollars I'd soon have in the bank with another eight hundred coming. I wanted to throw my arms around this man, but naturally I did no such thing. I thanked him, we shook hands formally, and I nodded at the receptionist as I left the office with my head in the clouds. Then I let out another joyous whoop and clattered across the wooden trestle to tell Beme the incredible news.

"Ha!" said Beme. "I knew you'd pull it off, kiddo. This calls for champagne."

We bought a bottle on the way to the camera shop and dashed up to the fifth floor to Earl's darkroom. Beme yanked out the cork, releasing a geyser of the fizzing golden liquid all over my fur jacket.

Word got around quickly via the corporate grapevine of my stunning pictures of the steel mill. Now everyone wanted my photographs. I got my own telephone line and no longer had to rely on the stationery store on the ground floor of my apartment house to take messages. Newspapers ordered my pictures for special features. Trade publications featured my photographs on their covers. Home and garden magazines asked for pictures of estates. I was confident that this was just the beginning.

Terminal Tower was already a landmark in downtown Cleveland. The Vans hired me as their official photographer with permission to go anywhere I chose, to highlight the grandeur of the great edifice but also to capture the intimate spaces. My prices climbed even higher. They were paying me a small fortune for my work, but I had to earn every penny of it.

I assembled a wardrobe of fashionable clothes, made to my design by a dressmaker. I visited a hairdresser regularly to keep my hair stylishly trimmed, bangs artfully curved above one eyebrow to flatter my eyes. My nails were manicured and lacquered in clear polish.

My pathetic little apartment with the bed that folded into the wall was obviously no place to meet clients. I needed an elegant studio. I showed up at the office of the agent in charge of renting suites in Terminal Tower and told him that I wanted a studio at the top of the tower.

He smiled at my boldness. "Sorry, Miss Bourke-White," he said, "the top floors belong to the Van Sweringens. Nobody, but *nobody*, lives on a higher floor than the Vans. However, I do have a place that I think would be just the thing for a lady of your accomplishments."

He escorted me to a suite on the twelfth floor with great views. Not as high as I wanted, but perfect, nevertheless. Now I had to negotiate a satisfactory rent. I talked him down as much as I could, and then I sweetly demanded certain concessions, like tiles and paint in my favorite colors. I ordered carpets, draperies that would set off my view of Public Square, a smoked glass tea table, and a plush armchair upholstered in silk mohair. Clients would feel so comfortable in that chair that they wouldn't be tempted to get up and walk away when I named my price for a series of photographs.

When everything was in place, I invited my mother and Roger to visit my new home. Roger whistled approvingly when he saw it. But Mother shook her head. "It's nice to know that you're doing well, Margaret, and that you're successful and you can afford all these . . . things. Even if you don't need them. But will they make you truly happy?"

I had hoped she would seem a little more excited, pleased, proud. Maybe that was too much to expect. "I don't know if it will make me happy. Right now, it's my work that makes me happy. And if it hadn't been for you buying me that secondhand camera, I wouldn't be here, Mother. I wouldn't have any of this. I can't thank you enough."

"All right, then," she said. "All right."

◆◆

When I wasn't putting in long hours on an assignment or spending whole nights in the darkroom, I began entertaining a steady stream of admirers—artists, architects, writers, businessmen—men I had met professionally who now wanted to go out with me. I enjoyed the company of men, and it was flattering to have so many men attracted to me. But I was not interested in romance. I was not quite twenty-four years old, and I'd made up my mind not to get fond of anyone until I was at least thirty. I wanted to establish myself in the next half-dozen years as a groundbreaking artist before I allowed myself to fall in love again.

In May of 1928, Mr. Kulas's favorite photograph of the enormous, overflowing ladle of molten steel took first place at a show at the Cleveland Museum of Art. Newspaper articles and magazine stories praised my work. I decided to throw a party to celebrate.

Wearing a beaded silk dress cut to show off my bare shoulders, I chatted with my guests as a waiter passed flutes of champagne and silver platters of hors d'oeuvres. One of my regular visitors arrived late. The maid, taking his hat, greeted him: "Good evening, Mr. Chapman."

Chappie bent down and kissed my cheek. "Hello, Peg. You're looking beautiful, as always. Congratulations."

My former husband and I had run into each other by accident when I was on assignment, and then we'd begun to meet occasionally for coffee. Now that we were no longer struggling with the burdens of marriage and his despicable mother, we'd managed to become friends. It amused us that none of my other visitors ever suspected our relationship. No one in Cleveland had any idea we had once been husband and wife.

"To Margaret Bourke-White, the most accomplished photographer in Cleveland!" cried a gentleman, raising his flute of champagne.

"The best anywhere!" shouted Chappie, and he caught my eye and winked.

21

New York, New York—1929

PHOTOGRAPHY WAS MY WHOLE LIFE. FOR TWO YEARS I explored Cleveland with my camera, capturing images of all kinds of industrial subjects—railroads, docks, mines—and it was paying off as my reputation grew. My work was in high demand. I charged high prices, and companies had plenty of money to pay for them.

I wasn't rich yet, but I was on my way. In May of 1929, I received a telegram from a man named Henry Luce, the publisher of a news magazine called *Time*. He had seen my steel-mill photographs, and he wanted to talk to me. "Request you come to New York soonest at our expense," he wired.

At first I wasn't much interested. I knew a little about *Time*, enough to notice that the only photograph in the magazine was a stuffy portrait of a boring politician on the cover. I didn't want to leave the work I was doing, and I didn't bother to reply to the telegram.

Later I began to reconsider. Here was the offer of a trip to New York, and even if nothing worked out with Mr. Luce and his magazine, I could call on architects around the city. Photographing buildings was where my career had begun back in

Ann Arbor, and my pictures of Terminal Tower in Cleveland had helped to cement my success. New York architecture was sure to be even more exciting. I packed up a portfolio of recent work and boarded a train to New York.

The *Time* offices were not impressive, but the two men I met there certainly were. Henry Luce was perhaps a half-dozen years older than me, broad-shouldered, with a fast and furious manner of talking. Leaping from subject to subject, he peppered me with questions about my background, my personal life, and my professional goals. I could hardly keep up with him.

Mr. Luce planned to launch a business magazine called *Fortune*, using elegantly composed photographs showing what I called patterns of industry. He boasted there was no other magazine like it. "You know what President Coolidge said: 'The business of America is business.' It's the right time to start a magazine like this, and you're the right person to take pictures for us."

The more he talked, the more I was intrigued by his ideas.

Parker Lloyd-Smith, the managing editor, spoke up. He was in his twenties, handsome as a Greek sculpture but better dressed. "I want to show your steel-mill pictures to potential advertisers as examples of the kind of quality we plan to feature in the magazine. Will you agree to that, Miss Bourke-White?"

"Of course."

"We want to hire you," said Mr. Luce. "The question is, can you start right away?"

I stalled for time, deciding how to reply. The Bourke-White Studio in Terminal Tower was very profitable. I hated to leave Cleveland, the business I had worked so hard to establish, and my suite in Terminal Tower. More importantly, I didn't want to be tied down by a full-time job.

Luce and Lloyd-Smith were waiting for an answer.

There was a knock on the door. "Yes?" barked Mr. Luce. A girl poked her sleek blond head into the office with a message. "Come on in, Ellie," he said. "I want you to meet Miss Bourke-White."

"Hello, Peggy," she said.

I looked at her sharply. The violet eyes seemed familiar. "This is our art director, Miss Treacy," Mr. Luce told me.

My jaw dropped. "Eleanor?"

Eleanor Treacy—crystal-chandelier girl, Madame Bol in the drama club play—extended her pale hand and smiled.

"You two know each other?" asked Mr. Luce.

"We were in the same class in high school," I explained.

"How nice that we may be working together, Peggy," said Eleanor, scanning me from head to toe. "I'm not sure I would have recognized you. You've become quite . . . chic."

What a delicious moment that was!

"Well, what do you say?" Mr. Luce demanded impatiently when she'd gone. "Will you come to work for us?"

I began replacing the photographs in my portfolio. "I need time to think about it, Mr. Luce," I said.

"Don't take too long," Mr. Luce growled, and I had the impression that he wasn't used to people who didn't jump when he said the word.

A few days later, back home in Cleveland, I wrote to Mr. Luce proposing that I work for him half time. I wanted a thousand dollars a month. It was a huge sum, and when two weeks passed with no reply, I thought I'd demanded too much. After a long delay, Parker Lloyd-Smith responded, saying that my proposal had been approved. A month later, in July of 1929, I went to work for *Fortune* and made the trip back to Cleveland between jobs.

My first assignment was to photograph shoe manufacturing in Lynn, Massachusetts; followed by glassmaking in Corning, New

York; then orchid-raising in New Jersey, and on to fisheries in Connecticut. Each time I was accompanied by a writer assigned to provide the text for the pictures and an assistant to haul my heavy equipment.

Sometimes my assistant was Mr. Luce himself. Harry—Mr. Luce had asked me to call him by his nickname—went with me to South Bend, Indiana, to work on an enormous project: "The Unseen Half of South Bend," documenting the entire city. He carried my cameras and once, when a ladle of molten metal spilled too near, dashed in and snatched the cameras from harm's way.

Since *Fortune* would not begin publication for another six months and many people had never even heard of *Time*, we were not treated like celebrities. Often we ended up joining a line of workers at a pushcart to grab a sandwich and coffee for lunch. Sometimes I was regarded as just another nuisance to be dealt with, not too different from my nights at Otis Steel.

I was on the road constantly. When I wasn't working for Mr. Luce, I took pictures for advertisers, who paid more than the magazine did. In October of 1929, a bank in Boston hired me to photograph the new lobby. I went to the bank on Thursday the twenty-fourth, planning to work all night, when I wouldn't be disturbed. But as I moved around the ornate lobby, selecting details, experimenting with the best angles, people continually rushed past, back and forth, getting in my way. This went on throughout the night interrupting shot after shot. I was exasperated. I stopped one of the clerks in mid-stride. "What's going on?" I demanded.

"The bottom has dropped out of the stock market! Haven't you been reading the papers?"

I hadn't. I rarely read newspapers, except for headlines. I frankly had no interest in world affairs or politics—all I was concerned with was my work. I just kept taking photographs. I had no idea that the Crash of '29 triggered that night was a financial disaster that would lead to the Great Depression and affect all of our lives. Especially mine.

◆◆

The assignments were never dull but they were anything but glamorous. The major feature *Fortune* assigned on the Chicago stockyards was an example.

It had been Parker Lloyd-Smith's idea, but a lot of his initial enthusiasm evaporated when we arrived at the Swift and Company meatpacking plant. Twenty thousand pigs were slaughtered there every single day.

Parker was in his fine clothes, carrying a notebook, and I had my mountains of cameras, tripods, cables, and lights. Hundreds of hogs were strung up by their hind hooves on a conveyor belt—Parker called it a "disassembly line." Each porker hung like the next in an endless repeating pattern, and patterns always attracted my eye. I took photograph after photograph, while Parker scribbled notes.

We spent several days photographing. On our last day we discovered a warehouse we hadn't yet explored. When we opened the door and peered in, an awful smell smacked us in the face. We stared at mountains of ochre-yellow dust. Parker reached for a linen handkerchief to hold over his nose.

"What *is* that?" Parker asked a worker.

"Pig dust."

Parker raised an eyebrow. "Pig dust? Meaning . . . ?"

"Well, you know what they say," drawled the worker, leaning on a shovel, "Swift uses every part of the pig but the squeal. You're looking at the scraps, the leftovers that can't even be made into sausage. It's ground up fine and mixed with meal for livestock feed."

"You mean, it's fed to other animals?" Parker looked queasy.

"Yeah. To other pigs."

"Good lord!" He backed out fast. "I'll wait in the car, Margaret," he called over his shoulder, and fled.

I set up my camera in the warehouse. The exposures had to be long, and I worked for over an hour. Parker must have thought I'd been overcome by the stench. But I got my pictures—piles of yellow pig dust resembling sand dunes that glowed in the filtered light.

These photographs were chosen for the lead story in the first issue of *Fortune*, and they helped to firmly establish my reputation. Photographers like Edward Weston used such simple objects as a pepper or a shell for his sensuous images. But I could find beauty even in something as disgusting as ground-up pig leavings.

◆◆

I loved being a trailblazer, not only in the field of photography but as a woman finding success in a man's world. I loved the attention, and I knew how to get even more of it. I began dressing entirely in black—silk, linen, cashmere—with one stunning piece of jewelry. I acquired a pair of elegant Afghan hounds and took them for walks in Public Square whenever I was in Cleveland, but I traveled so much that the dogs suffered from neglect, and I had to give them to a friend. Sometimes I carried a silver-headed walking stick, until I decided that it was a nuisance. I enjoyed having men make it a point to be with me because it made them feel important to be seen with a glamorous and accomplished woman. That plain old linsey-woolsey girl of high school days could now have practically any man she wanted.

But I didn't want a man.

I was afraid that, like my walking stick, he might get in my way. Maybe he'd be jealous of my work, object when an assignment kept me out all night or took me away for days or weeks. He might believe my place was at home, caring for the children, caring for *him*. Maybe he wouldn't put up with me working with other men. I was twenty-five, and I decided that someday, when I was in my thirties, if the right man came along, then I might risk falling in love again. Meanwhile each new assignment absorbed all my attention.

◆ ◆

When the stock market crashed in the fall of 1929, the wealthy people I worked for did not seem to be concerned. Mr. Walter Chrysler was one of those people. After I was hired to photograph the Chrysler automobile assembly line in Detroit, my pictures came to his attention. Mr. Chrysler was building a skyscraper in New York, and he wanted its construction to be documented week by week.

Summoned to his New York office, I assumed I would meet with an underling, so I was surprised when Mr. Chrysler greeted me. A shaggy-browed man with a reputation for a fearsome temper, he greeted me with a smile.

"Let me tell you something, Miss Bourke-White," Mr. Chrysler said. "I intend for this to be the tallest building in the country, maybe in the world. You've got that Terminal Tower in Cleveland, seven hundred and seventy-one feet high. The Bank of Manhattan is nine hundred twenty-seven feet high. And now the Empire State Building is going up—more competition. I had the Chrysler Building designed to reach one thousand forty-six feet. I need photographs taken at every stage to show that the steel tower on the top is an integral part of the structure, and not just a decoration stuck on to claim the title of 'tallest.' Will you do it?"

He pushed the architectural drawings across the conference table and leaned back, watching me keenly. I looked at the drawings and knew instantly that I wanted to do it. "Of course," I said.

What a rough job I'd let myself in for! All through the winter months of 1930, I worked in temperatures that regularly dropped well below freezing. My fingers stiffened and my eyes watered. I sometimes climbed a long, unfinished stairway and perched in a tower, eight hundred feet above the ground, that swayed in the wind, several feet in one direction and then in another. It took three men to hold the tripod for my camera. I was not afraid of heights, but at first the swaying unnerved me. One of the riveters taught me to remember how I felt walking along fence tops as a child. It worked. The experience was exhilarating.

Enormous stainless steel gargoyles in the shape of eagles' heads glared down at the ant-sized pedestrians sixty-one floors below. I fell in love with the Chrysler Building, and I wanted an apartment near one of those gargoyles. It was time to give up my studio in Cleveland. I was still making plenty of money, even as the Depression worsened the lives of many people, and I could afford to make New York my base.

I submitted my application to the rental agent, who said sympathetically, "Sorry, Miss Bourke-White, but private persons cannot live in office buildings. It's a New York City law." Then he added, "The only person permitted to live in an office building is the janitor."

"Is that so?" I thanked him and left, returning an hour later with a neatly typed application for employment—as janitor of the Chrysler Building. I had exaggerated my qualifications somewhat, but I could hire people who had the skills to maintain the building. It wouldn't be a problem. I knew I could pull it off.

The rental agent glanced at my application. "You're serious?"

"Of course I'm serious." I tapped the paper on his desk. "You may check my references." At the top of the list was Mr. Walter

Percy Chrysler, president of the Chrysler Corporation.

"I'm sorry to have to tell you, ma'am, but the position has already been filled."

Legally, I could not live there, but I knew how to get around the city law: make the apartment a workplace, not a home. I rented space on the sixty-first floor, next to one of the gorgeous gargoyles, and hired a designer to transform it into a studio, all graceful curves and dramatic angles with an aquarium for tropical fish built into one wall.

Now I had to get enough big assignments to pay the rent on my fabulous—and fabulously expensive—penthouse studio.

◆◆

After the first edition of *Fortune* came out in February 1930, featuring my photographs of the meatpacking plant, my name became well known by the richest and most powerful people in the country. After that, every issue of *Fortune* featured at least one, and sometimes several, Margaret Bourke-White photographs. Early in my life I had announced my ambition: to be rich and famous. I was now well on my way. Not often, but once in a while, I stopped and dared to ask myself, *Are you happy, Margaret?* I had every reason to be—I was achieving everything I'd dreamed of.

But I had few true friends. I confided in no one. I liked men, and a great many male admirers were always pleased to be in my company. There was no time to develop the kind of friendships with women I'd once had with Madge at Barnard and Camp Agaming, or with Tubby and Sara Jane back in high school. I had almost no contact with my sister, Ruth, who was unmarried and still working and living in Chicago. In fact I didn't much *like* women. I thought they lived dull lives, and they were inevitably jealous of me, my success, my exciting life.

Sometimes I thought of the people I'd left behind in

Cleveland. Beme, for instance, and Earl, who had cheered me on. I often missed them.

My mother did not fail to let me know what she thought of the life I was leading. "I'm proud of your accomplishments, Margaret," she told me before I gave up my studio in Cleveland and left permanently for New York. "But I worry about your values. I see that you've become self-indulgent. The clothes, the jewelry and expensive furniture, and those silly dogs. Such personal display does not become you. And that automobile!"

I had replaced Patrick with an almost-new Nash roadster. "Mother, I need a car to haul my equipment," I explained.

I tried to dismiss her criticisms, but nevertheless, they stung.

22

From Russia to the Dust Bowl—1930

By the summer of 1930 I was spending half the year in the crazy world of advertising, where I could make the most money, and the other half working for *Fortune*, where I found the most satisfaction. After I'd wound up the Chrysler project, Harry decided to send me to Germany to photograph that country's thriving industries. I had another idea: I wanted to go to Russia—the Soviet Union, as it was now called.

Russia's Five-Year Plan, launched two years earlier, was intended to turn an agricultural country into an industrialized nation able to compete with the United States. Communist collectives replaced peasants' farms, and factories with production quotas sprang up all across the huge country. I wanted to be the first American to photograph the changes.

"You'll never get in," Harry said when I proposed the idea. "Foreigners aren't welcome in Russia—especially foreigners with cameras. Focus your energy on Germany."

There was nothing like a closed door to make me want to pry it open.

At the Russian tourist bureau in New York I asked if I'd need any special visas to visit Russia. "Your photographs will be your passport," said the official in charge who recognized my name and knew my work. "The Russians will love your pictures. The sweep! The grandeur! Your style is so—so *Russian!*" I took his response to mean that I'd have no problems getting permission.

Harry gave in, and Parker Lloyd-Smith and I sailed to Germany on the SS *Brémen* and went to work on our assignment. For almost six weeks, as we moved from town to town photographing German factories, I waited anxiously for word that the paperwork had been approved and I had permission to go on to Russia. Weeks passed without any sign of my visa.

In the meantime I was running into problems in Germany. Not every factory would allow a woman inside to take photographs. One day, while I was setting up my cameras in a wheat field to take a picture of a line of smokestacks on the horizon, the police swooped in and arrested me. I was accused of being a spy. Even when the State Department in Washington wrote in my defense, the police refused to release me. Frantic, but also inspired, I showed them my pictures of those hogs in the Chicago stockyards. That convinced them I was not a spy and let me go.

Parker Lloyd-Smith left for New York. It was one of the last times I saw him before he died the next year. I worried that I would have to leave too. After weeks of anxiety my visa came through, but now I faced another challenge. Russia had been in the grip of a famine since the farms were collectivized, and food was scarce. Veteran travelers warned me to take my own.

I packed a trunk with cans of beans, meat, cheese, and whatever else I could think of and caught a train to Moscow. I hired a young woman as an interpreter, and for weeks we traveled thousands of miles across the country, living on my cache of canned goods and dealing with endless tangles of red tape.

With every request to go somewhere, see someone, or

photograph something, I was told, "Come back the day after tomorrow, and it will be taken care of." I learned that in Russia it was always "the day after tomorrow." I'd set up an appointment to photograph a factory and then worry about how I'd get there. If my interpreter and I were lucky enough to find a taxi, it was likely to break down. Or we took a droshky, a carriage drawn by an exhausted horse. Or we crowded onto a streetcar and then did not have the proper fare. Once at my destination, I was usually told that the proper paperwork had not arrived, or the person in charge had the day off, or the manufacturing schedule now made interruptions for photographs out of the question. "Come back the day after tomorrow." And I did, over and over, until I got my photographs.

I took pictures of blast furnaces in operation and dams under construction, and I met workers curious about America. They loved the conveyor belts and assembly lines that made our country so productive. They were also curious about *me*. A group of women assembling telegraph machines gathered around me at the end of their shift to admire my pictures and ask questions through my interpreter.

"Ladies want to know if you have husband," she reported.

I smiled and shook my head. "*Nyet*," I said, one of a few words of Russian I'd picked up.

"Ladies want to know if you are in love."

"Only with my camera," I told them, laughing. Shaking their heads, they went back to work, and so did I.

❖ ❖

By 1932, America was mired deep in the Great Depression. Millions of people were out of work, destitute, and with no way to feed their families. But I was still making lots of money, and I enjoyed spending it. I loved beautiful clothes, and the clothes I loved—suits from Paris, for example—were expensive. But the more assignments I got, the more people I had to hire, and the higher my expenses climbed. Suddenly, reality caught up with me. Many of my advertising clients could not pay what they owed me, and I fell behind on the rent on my glamorous penthouse studio in the Chrysler Building. I'd been paying my brother's expenses since he started classes at Ohio State, fulfilling my promise to the Mungers to help another student in need, but when he transferred to MIT, I couldn't keep up. I had to turn to Uncle Lazar for help, and I hated that.

I was working as hard as ever to try to keep my head above water, but like many others I was in debt to almost everybody, and I was broke and desperate. My charge accounts were being closed. I borrowed money from friends and even from Mother, who was also in tight circumstances. I asked her to sell the roadster for me in Cleveland where I'd left it. I moved out of the Chrysler Building penthouse to a cheaper studio on Fifth Avenue. Soon I owed back rent there as well. When an official came around with an eviction notice, I avoided him until I could scrape together what I owed.

It wasn't just the Depression that brought hard times to the country. During the summer of 1934, people were talking about the so-called Dust Bowl in the Great Plains of the Midwest. Farmers had plowed up the soil, destroying the native grasses, a prolonged drought had allowed the topsoil to dry out, and now windstorms blew the loose soil in great suffocating clouds. In New York we heard about it, but nobody understood the extent of it. Ralph Ingersoll, who took over as *Fortune*'s managing editor after Parker's death, assigned me to fly to Omaha to document the growing catastrophe.

"You have three hours to pack, Margaret," Ralph growled. "And I want the story in five days."

The huge swath of devastation stretching from the Texas

Panhandle to the Dakotas was much larger than any of us back East had ever imagined, and five days gave me very little time. I hired a beat-up plane and a beat-up barnstorming pilot to fly it. We covered the vast expanse, jumping from one desolate spot to the next in blistering sun and relentless wind, flying low over mile after mile of baked earth, dry riverbeds, withered corn, and blowing dust that buried everything in its path. I had no time to speak to anyone, but I photographed it all. The gaunt faces etched with despair told the wordless story and affected me deeply.

That experience changed the way I saw the world. When I'd first begun taking pictures of abstract industrial patterns, I sometimes included people to give a sense of scale. The photograph of a man working near a turbine illustrated its hugeness, but the man himself was of no interest to me then. Now it was *people* who mattered.

For the next two years, from 1934 to 1936, back in the hard-edged world of advertising, I photographed tires for Goodyear and automobiles for Buick, two accounts that paid some of my bills. I did not want to do any more elaborately staged photographs for magazine advertisers, even when they offered me a thousand dollars a picture. I certainly needed the money. I resolved that once I had paid off the bill collectors, I would do only photographic work that was truly important, that meant something. I wasn't sure what that would be.

Then, in the summer of 1936, two years after my transforming trip to the Dust Bowl, my life and my work were brought into sharp focus by a sad and painful event: my mother's death. Sixty-two and in good health, she had come to New York to take a summer class at Columbia. With no warning, she had a heart attack and died. As I mourned, I realized how central she had been to my life, even though I had not realized it at the time. My mother's death helped to crystallize my goals.

I could not forget the faces of the people and the misery I'd witnessed in the Dust Bowl. I vowed to do a book about ordinary Americans. As a photographer I was second to no one, but I didn't have much experience as a writer. I needed someone first-class with whom to collaborate. But what sort of writer would that be—a novelist or journalist? Someone famous, or some as-yet-unknown talent? He would have to be as serious about the project as I was, and as fully committed to bringing a portrait of America to a wide audience. I felt sure I would recognize him when I met him. It would be intuitive: I would meet a writer, and we would look at each other, and we would both *know*.

And that is exactly what happened.

Skinny and Kit—1936

"YOU SHOULD READ ERSKINE CALDWELL'S BOOK," a literary agent named Maxim Lieber advised me when we met at a party. "He wrote *Tobacco Road* as a novel about the South, and he's thinking about going back to Georgia with a photographer and doing something different."

I had heard about Erskine Caldwell and *Tobacco Road*, describing the awful plight of poor white sharecroppers in rural Georgia. The book, published four years earlier in 1932, still had people talking, not just because of the sex and the immoral characters, but because many readers insisted that his portrayal of the South and Southerners was all wrong. They said it painted a distorted picture of the inhabitants and their wretched lives. The book had been made into a Broadway show that was played for laughs and still drew big crowds.

"I want to meet him," I told Lieber.

I bought *Tobacco Road* the next day and read it straight through. The story of Jeeter Lester and the often grotesque characters was raw and shocking. It took a strong stomach to read parts of the book, but the clear, unsentimental prose transported me to rural Georgia. The book had been banned in some places, and the New York Society for the Suppression of Vice, a self-appointed group, had tried unsuccessfully to have him arrested at a book signing.

I called Lieber and asked if he'd mentioned me to Caldwell.

"Yeah," Lieber said, "I have. He's willing to meet with you. I'm not supposed to tell you this, but Erskine isn't crazy about your pictures."

"There are plenty of my pictures I don't much care for either," I said. "But when you're working in advertising, you often have to do things you don't like. That's one of the reasons I want to do this book. I'm sick of the commercial stuff. I want to do something that really matters."

"There's more, Margaret," said the agent, "and you might as well hear it now, before you're in too deep. Erskine doesn't like the idea of working with a woman."

I laughed. "I've heard that one before from men who didn't want me to go into their steel mills or down into their mines. But they got over it. Mr. Caldwell will get over it, too."

Caldwell had recently written a series of newspaper articles about Southern sharecroppers and taken his own pictures. I looked them up. The pictures weren't much good, but the writing was vivid and powerful. I had no intention of letting Mr. Caldwell's hesitance stop me from doing what I wanted to do. If he refused, I'd find another writer, but I was confident he would not. I called Lieber again. "Has Mr. Caldwell made up his mind?"

"He has tentatively agreed, but he wants to meet you before he gives a firm yes."

We met in Lieber's office in February. I arrived early, and Lieber had just enough time to tell me that his client had overcome some of his doubts about me. Erskine Caldwell was a large man with blue eyes, reddish hair, freckles, a courtly manner, and a soft Southern accent. He seemed shy. I knew that Southern men did not like to be approached head-on, so I took an indirect angle.

"Mr. Caldwell, I admire your work tremendously," I purred, "and I would consider it a very great honor if you would consent to help me with a project that is so close to my heart." Honey dripped from my lips.

Erskine nodded soberly. "And I would be honored to work with such a talented woman."

Now we could talk seriously. With prodding from Lieber and me, we settled a few things. We would drive throughout the Deep South. Erskine would bring along his literary secretary, Sally, to take notes. He was involved in a few projects that he needed to finish up first, and we would leave in five months, on June eleventh.

The delay suited me well. I, too, had unfinished business with advertising clients. We shook hands and went our separate ways.

Not long after that meeting with Erskine, Harry Luce greeted me with exciting news: he was preparing to launch another magazine, a weekly that would feature photographs. He wanted me to play a leading role, although exactly what wasn't yet clear. Harry and the rest of the team were in the frantic process of putting together dummies of the magazine to show to potential advertisers. They aimed to put out the first issue that fall.

The new magazine's name was *Life*. I had one assignment locked up: documenting the life cycle of the praying mantis. That took me back to my early interest in the natural world and the children's book I'd once worked on and then abandoned.

The five months since my first—and only—conversation with Erskine Caldwell flew by. We had agreed to begin our joint venture on June eleventh, but now I had several additional things to attend to. June came and went, and I needed to postpone the trip. I assumed that Erskine's life was as hectic as mine, and that a delay of a few days, even weeks, would not be a big issue.

I was wrong. I had no idea that my collaborator was a stickler for dates and deadlines. When I couldn't reach Erskine, I called Maxim Lieber.

"He's already left for Georgia," said Lieber.

"Where is he?" I cried. "How can I reach him? This is too important! I can't just let this go!"

"He's in Wrens, the little town where he grew up. He's at his father's home."

I began to weep. "Maxim, please! Is there a phone? You've got to give me the number!"

Maxim sighed. "I promised never to give out this number." Then he gave it to me.

Erskine answered the phone. Still in tears, I begged for just a little more time. The previously soft-spoken Southern gentleman snapped, "Very well, Miss Bourke-White, the project is hereby postponed—indefinitely!" And hung up on me.

I was stunned. Surely he couldn't mean it! But his icy voice and abrupt words didn't bode well for the outcome. I could not bear to let that happen. I would go to Wrens, Georgia, wherever that was, and change his mind.

I always kept clothes and camera equipment packed so that I could leave on short notice, but I had to be prepared to travel with Erskine for who knew how long. Since I would be working on my photo-essay on praying mantises while I was away, I added two large glass jars, each containing a twig with an egg case to my luggage. They were due to hatch soon, and I had to be ready.

At midnight that night I boarded a plane for Georgia and arrived in Augusta at sunrise. While the bellhop carried up my luggage, I sat in the hotel coffee shop and composed a letter to Erskine, emphasizing how serious I was about the project. I set off for the post office. At eight o'clock the sun was already blazing, and my dress was soaked with perspiration. The mail would not go out until late that afternoon, I was told, and would not be delivered until Monday.

"How far is it to Wrens?" I asked.

The postmaster scratched his bald head. "'Bout six miles, I reckon."

Sick with disappointment, I stepped out onto the sun-blasted sidewalk. A young lad was rearranging the dust on the post office steps. I noticed a bicycle leaning against a tree.

"I'll pay you five dollars if you'll take this to Wrens," I said, giving him the letter.

It must have seemed like a small fortune, and the boy leaped onto the bicycle and pedaled away, stirring up clouds of dust.

I had done all I could, and now there was nothing to do but wait. And hope.

I went up to my room and took a cool bath and changed my clothes, went back downstairs, and settled in a rocking chair on the broad porch of the hotel.

The hours dragged by. Not even the hint of a breeze stirred as the sun made its lazy arc across the Georgia sky. I longed to find a shady side of the street and explore the city, but I did not dare leave my post except to revisit the coffee shop for lunch.

The afternoon passed, and I remained a prisoner, chained to my rocking chair. Around six o'clock Erskine climbed the steps to the porch. "Coffee?" he asked.

I followed him to the coffee shop—my third time that day—and took the stool next to his at the counter. We ordered. Erskine studied his thumbs. Neither of us spoke. Two cups of coffee arrived, and we drank them in silence. The waitress took away our empty cups. Erskine paid.

"Quite an argument we had, wasn't it?" he asked, poker-faced.

"Um-hmm." I kept a straight face, too.

"When will you be ready to leave?"

"I'm ready now."

Erskine called for the bellhop to fetch the bags from my room. I was warning the boy to be careful of the glass jars when a taxi pulled up in front of the hotel and a woman stepped out and joined us. "This is Sally, my literary secretary," Erskine said off-handedly. "She'll be invaluable." Sally was thin and angular with sharp features. Her small, bright eyes swept over me from head to toe. Erskine went off to help the bellhop load my bags into his car.

When he reappeared, Sally climbed into the backseat, and we drove to Wrens. It turned out to be thirty miles from Augusta, not a half-dozen. In Wrens, Erskine added his luggage to mine, Sally smoked silently, and I made small talk with Erskine's father, a retired preacher.

When we were ready, the secretary wedged herself into the crevice between mountains of gear in the backseat. I asked to make one last check on the glass jars with the egg cases, and as I did, the lid of the trunk came down on my head with a painful whack. Erskine laughed—*laughed!*—and said he hoped something funny like that happened every day. I suppose he thought he was being witty. I should have recognized then that this man would be a difficult traveling companion.

Heading southwest from Augusta and following back roads, we drove for several hours without anyone saying a word. Erskine reminded me of my father and the long silences that sometimes infuriated my mother. Sometime after midnight we reached a small, nameless town with a small, rundown building that passed itself off as a hotel and was, by some miracle, still open. We booked three rooms with rusted plumbing and threadbare towels. A creaking ceiling fan stirred the humid air. Without bothering to undress, I lay down on top of the faded pink chenille spread and fell instantly asleep.

It seemed I had scarcely closed my eyes when I was

awakened by a pounding on my door. "Rise and shine! Up and at 'em! Time to hit the road!"

Erskine, it turned out, was an early riser, no matter how late he'd been up the night before. Sally was already supervising the reloading of the car. I gulped some toast and coffee with barely time to brush my teeth, and we were off. We followed dirt roads that wandered through cotton country in which Erskine was completely at home and I felt as though I had just been transported to some foreign land.

So it went for the next few days. Erskine and I got on each other's nerves. We argued almost constantly. We were too different. He seemed to think he was in charge of our project and would make the decisions for both of us. I, naturally, assumed that I was in charge of the photography, period, and he would have nothing to say about how I set up my pictures. As he talked to his subjects—a farmer and his wife, say—in the most off-hand way, I lurked in the background with a small camera, trying not to be noticed. I took background shots of crumbling barns, or the interiors of unpainted shacks with newspapers pasted on the walls to keep out the winter cold. I captured small details, such as an abandoned plow. And I photographed the people when they were not expecting it.

By the fourth day, I had been reduced to tears as many times. I'd always had the habit of weeping when I felt pushed to the wall, and Erskine was pushing and pushing. He believed I was "turning on the waterworks," as he put it, on purpose, as a way to manipulate him. This was not true. I simply could not bear to have anyone trying to control me, and I reacted by bursting into tears.

On the fifth day we drove into Arkansas, and the project threatened to blow up. Erskine came to my room to help me carry my equipment out to the car—he was always the chivalrous Southern gentleman in such matters—but instead of picking up my tripod and camera cases, he perched on the windowsill and gazed at me for a long, uncomfortable moment. "Margaret," he said, "I need to have a talk with you."

I was about to pack my toothbrush. "About what?"

"About what we're doing. This is not going to work. I think we should forget the whole thing. It's been a mistake. You go your way, and I'll go mine. No hard feelings."

Still holding my toothbrush, I sank down on the bed. "Erskine, you don't understand. This book means everything to me. When I saw the Dust Bowl, I began to realize that people are more than just figures in the background. My whole direction has changed. This book is the most important work I've done in my life, and I can't give it up!"

"You could go on and do it on your own. You don't need me."

"But I do! I do need you!" And there I was, weeping again, huddled on the edge of the bed, my face buried in my hands. Erskine got up from the windowsill and moved toward me. I reached up to him, tears pouring down my cheeks, and he pulled me into his arms and kissed me, my eyes, my wet face, my lips.

Everything was different after those kisses. I had not realized how strongly I was drawn to him, probably had been from the first time we met. A few weeks before we began the trip I had observed my thirty-second birthday, two years past the deadline I'd set for falling in love. Perhaps that's what was now happening. My work was changing, opening me up, and apparently so was my heart. I was wary, certain I did not want to be dominated or controlled. But oh, the powerful attraction I felt for Erskine! Now I acknowledged it, even though I knew he was married with a wife in Maine, and children too.

Sally undoubtedly sensed what was happening between us. We didn't do anything to hide it, and I had suspected from the first that Sally herself was in love with him. That night in the wee hours she packed up and left our seedy hotel outside of Pine Bluff. We found the note the next morning.

She couldn't stand sitting in the backseat, stuck between all our gear, she wrote. She couldn't stand traveling with the two of us. Maybe one temperamental writer could be borne, or one equally temperamental photographer, but *both*? Crowded into the same automobile in the middle of a hot Arkansas summer? It was simply too much! She was going home to California.

From then on, it was just the two of us.

I admired Erskine's relaxed, easy manner with the people we met. With his soft Southern drawl, he sounded like one of them, and he knew exactly how to talk to them and ask simple questions about their lives. They trusted him completely from the start.

But I was different. My accent marked me as a Yankee and an outsider, and people in these parts, the poorest-of-the-poor sharecroppers, didn't trust "foreigners." It was an effort for me not to try to arrange everything and everyone. I set up shots to please my eye, rather than to record things as they really were.

"Slow down a little," he told me. "You're coming on like the Vandals and the Visigoths."

It took a while, but eventually, because of Erskine, people began to trust me and my camera, too. I knew I was doing good work. We both were.

Erskine began calling me Kit. "You look like a kitten that's just drunk a bowl of cream," he said, stroking my hair. "It suits you better than Peg or Maggie."

I started calling him Skinny, because he wasn't.

◆◆

The two glass jars with the praying mantis egg cases now rode with me in the front seat of Erskine's Ford. The eggs might start to hatch at any time, whenever the temperature and humidity were exactly right. We were bouncing down a dirt road past fields of cotton when I checked the glass jars and saw the first nymphs wriggle out of an egg case. "Pull over, Skinny!" I ordered. "They're hatching!"

Erskine stopped, and I quickly set up my equipment and placed the egg cases on a fence rail. My camera and tripod always attracted an audience, and as I began taking pictures, a dozen or so children appeared out of nowhere and surrounded me. We all watched, spellbound, as hundreds of tiny nymphs poured out of the egg cases, clambering over each other on legs as thin as threads.

"They look like little devil horses!" cried one enchanted boy. Some of the "little devil horses" began eating their brothers, a habit that bothered Erskine but didn't trouble the children.

The surviving nymphs went back into the jars, and for the next several days I recorded each stage of their development from tiny nymph to full-grown mantis, shedding their exoskeletons and forming new ones as they continued to grow, perhaps as many as ten times, until they reached adult size. It had been so long since I'd worked on my children's book about insects that I'd almost forgotten how much I enjoyed photographing the natural world.

At the end of August Erskine and I were back in New York. We'd accomplished what we'd set out to do, but there was still more to be done. We talked about returning to the South—we just weren't sure when. I'd finished my photo-essay on the life cycle of the praying mantis for *Life*, and I'd signed an exclusive contract to work for the new magazine.

That fall Harry Luce handed me an assignment, to appear in the first issue: photographing the Fort Peck Dam under construction along the Missouri River in Montana.

"They're claiming the dam will be the largest of its kind," said Harry Luce. "I hear it's a monster. President Roosevelt's idea for giving jobs to upwards of a thousand jobless men." He looked up at me from beneath his bushy eyebrows. "Keep your eye open for something that might make a great cover. And while you're there, take a look at the shantytowns that seem to be springing up everywhere. You have two weeks."

I packed my equipment and prepared to leave as I'd done many times before. But this time was different: Erskine and I had fallen deeply in love, and going away was harder than I'd expected. It was quite a new sensation for me, and he made no secret of how much it bothered him when I said good-bye to him in New York and headed out alone for Montana.

Roosevelt's Dam and a Flood—1936

My destination was the brand-new town of New Deal, named for the president's program to help the country recover from the Depression. I rented a tiny spare room in a school-teacher's trailer and went to work.

The dam was an almost impossibly enormous engineering project. I set up my camera to photograph it with two workmen in the foreground, looking no bigger than my thumb, to suggest the dam's mammoth size. This was the kind of work I'd done many times before, so different from the book I was working on with Erskine, but still exciting.

The dam was made of compacted earth pumped up from the river bottom. I photographed the earthworks and the equipment that was creating it in the early mornings when the light was good. In the afternoons, when the light was too flat to take pictures, I explored on horseback the area that would become a water-filled reservoir when the dam was completed. But in my off-hours I wandered through the ramshackle town, stopping in at the Bar X and the Buck Horn Club where men and women of New Deal passed their evenings. I'd learned from Erskine how to talk to people, earning their trust, before I shot pictures.

Some of the men didn't much like having a camera pointed at them and let me know it. "Whoa there, little lady, how 'bout you just put that camera away, there's a good girl."

The taxi dancers, girls who were paid to dance with the fellows who asked them, didn't like it either.

"I don't want my mum to see my picture and know what I'm doing," one girl told me, turning away to hide her face. "She thinks I'm a secretary."

"But you're not doing anything wrong," I said. "A dance is just a dance."

"Don't try to tell *her* that. She'd think I was no better than one of them ladies of the evening."

If someone objected, I put away my camera, but if no one did, I kept shooting.

I received a wire from Wilson Hicks, *Life*'s picture editor back in New York. He wanted to include a section to be called "*Life* Goes to a Party." The deadline for the first issue was approaching. Did I have anything they could use? I wired back that I had just what they might be looking for, and along with photographs of the dam I shipped off pictures of New Deal night life—the drinkers, the taxi dancers, even the waitress's little daughter perched on the bar at the saloon. Hicks may have been surprised by the photographs I sent, so different from anything else I'd done, but he used them for the first "Party" feature.

My photograph of the dam was chosen to be the cover of the inaugural issue of *Life*. It hit the newsstands on November 19 and sold out within hours. The printers could not keep up with the orders.

◆◆

I loved working for *Life*. I loved Skinny. There were problems. One fact could not be changed: Erskine was married but

Margaret's dramatic photograph of Fort Peck Dam was Life magazine's first cover.

separated from his wife. At first we tried to keep our love affair a secret, but soon everyone guessed. I had given up the Fifth Avenue studio when I could not afford it any longer and moved into an apartment on East Forty-Second Street. Erskine kept a room at the Mayfair Hotel on West Forty-Ninth, but we were together constantly—unless I was away on an assignment. And that created tension. I loved him, but I valued my work every bit as much as I valued him.

Erskine was not used to being with a truly independent woman, and it rattled him. I felt that he wanted to tie me down. When he brought up the subject of marriage, I always put him off. I didn't want to marry him—I didn't want to marry, *period*—because I knew deep in my bones that marriage didn't suit me. I had a different kind of life, a life built around my work, and that was how I wanted it.

"Darling, you already have a wife," I reminded him. "You're married to Helen, remember? So there's no point in even discussing it."

"Of course we can discuss it! And we ought to! I'll get a divorce, and then it will all be settled."

I didn't believe marriage would settle anything. Still, he kept bringing up the subject, and I kept refusing to discuss it.

◆ ◆

In January of 1937, two months after *Life*'s first issue, the Ohio River was inundating Louisville, Kentucky, in one of the most damaging floods in American history. My editor dispatched me to cover it. I had an hour to get ready.

Erskine was dismayed. "You're leaving again, Kit? When will you be back?"

"When I've finished shooting," I said over my shoulder. I was busy making sure I had enough film, enough bulbs, enough toothpaste. I was already thinking about my new assignment.

"I wish you weren't going," he said, hovering nearby. "I miss you when you're not here." We had been together as a couple for months by then, and he still seemed distressed when I went away.

"I miss you, too, Skinny, but this is what I do. You know that." I finished packing and snapped my bag shut. "The taxi's waiting. I'll call you as soon as I can."

Erskine helped carry down my gear, the cabbie loaded it into the trunk, and I jumped into the backseat. Erskine leaned in. "Don't I even deserve a kiss?"

"Of course, darling," I said. I admit it was not much of a kiss. "I've got a plane to catch."

As the driver pulled away from the curb, I glanced back and saw Erskine standing forlornly on the sidewalk, hands plunged into his pockets. I felt uneasy, leaving him like that, and I was about to order the cab to turn back, so I could kiss him properly. But then the cab turned the corner, and I was headed for the airport, away from Skinny and bound for Kentucky.

◆ ◆

I was on the last plane to land at the Louisville airport before it was submerged along with most of the city. But how would I get into town with my camera and equipment when everything was surrounded by floodwaters?

I spotted a rowboat and stuck out my thumb.

"Where you going, miss?" shouted one of the rowers.

"Downtown to the newspaper office."

"We're not going that far, but we'll take you as far as we can."

I scrambled into the boat next to supplies of food and water they were taking to a neighborhood that was marooned. Along the way the rowers stopped to rescue people clinging desperately to tree branches or perched on floating bits of furniture. I was afraid to unpack my cameras for fear the boat would be swamped. But I couldn't think of the excellent picture possibilities I would miss.

When a good-sized raft came along, the rowers flagged it down. Struggling to keep my gear from getting soaked, I clambered from the rowboat onto the raft and managed to take pictures of floodwaters surging through the streets. At the offices of the *Courier-Journal,* exhausted reporters who had descended on Louisville to document the disaster were sleeping on desks or on the floor, and I crept among them, snapping pictures of them, too.

As the floodwaters began to recede, I grabbed my camera and went out on the streets. I found a relief center where clothing and supplies were being doled out. Dozens of Negroes waited in line with empty sacks and buckets in front of a gigantic billboard proclaiming, *WORLD'S HIGHEST STANDARD OF LIVING.* A smiling white family in a shiny new car—father, mother, two children, and a pooch—grinned beneath the slogan *There's no way like the American Way.*

My shot of the weary Negroes with dazed expressions captured the bitter irony of that slogan. It was featured in the lead story in the next issue of *Life.*

◆◆

When I returned from Louisville, all was forgiven, and Erskine and I went back to work on the book we had started the summer before. By the time we made a second trip south later that spring to finish the job, we had hit on a way to work together: I took pictures without his interference, Erskine wrote text without mine, and we wrote the captions for the pictures together. We'd lay eight photographs on the floor and study them, we'd each write a caption and later we'd compare the two. Sometimes we combined the results, or used my idea and Erskine's words, or the other way around. We made a good team.

We had not talked about a title until the day we delivered the manuscript and photographs to the editor. While we waited to see him, Erskine said, "The title is *You Have Seen Their Faces.* What do you think, Kit? Do you like it?"

I thought it captured exactly what we'd been working so hard to say. I took his face in my two hands and kissed him on the mouth, not giving a fig what the steely-faced receptionist might think. "It's perfect," I said, and kissed him again.

I also believed it was the most important work I'd ever done, and I was ready for the challenge of another book. I was also ready for the next exciting assignment from *Life*. It came in July, when I was dispatched to cover several stories in the Arctic. I was thrilled. What an adventure! Erskine, of course, was not pleased at all.

"How long will you be gone this time, Kit?" he asked peevishly.

"As long as it takes, darling," I promised, "and not a day longer."

Overleaf: Margaret's photograph captures the irony of flood survivors waiting beneath a cheerful billboard.

25

The Arctic—1937

Lᴏʀᴅ Tᴡᴇᴇᴅsᴍᴜɪʀ, ᴀ ɴᴀᴛɪᴠᴇ Sᴄᴏᴛ ʀᴇᴄᴇɴᴛʟʏ appointed governor general of Canada, had set himself the goal of touring the width and breadth of the huge and diverse country for which he was now responsible. His Excellency was believed to be traveling aboard an old steamer somewhere in the vast Canadian tundra, heading north. My editors at *Life* decided this had the makings of "a cracking good story"—if I could find him.

I spent a day or two in Edmonton, the capital of the province of Alberta, making the rounds of bars and cafes and asking questions until I found a bush pilot who'd heard of the governor general's tour. I hired him, and he loaded me and my equipment, which included a suitcase with the chrysalises of a dozen butterflies, into a small pontoon plane. I was still working on what had become a long-term project of photographing the metamorphoses of various insects, and I'd brought them with me.

We took off in search of His Excellency's boat, the *Distributor*. "It's probably on the Athabasca River headed toward the Northwest Territories, loaded with supplies for trappers. That's my guess," the pilot shouted above the noisy engine.

For nearly three hours we followed the course of the river, skimming above the tundra, around jutting mountain ranges, and over shimmering lakes, until we sighted the steamer. The pilot swooped in low and dropped down beside it. My cameras and I were hoisted aboard, the pilot flew off, and the *Distributor* continued to churn steadily upstream, hour after hour, with stops at tiny villages and hamlets along the way. At each stop Lord Tweedsmuir stepped off the boat briefly and delivered his greetings, exactly the same each time, in a nearly impenetrable Scottish brogue that left his subjects glassy-eyed.

I took photographs of the scenery as the *Distributor* wended its way through the tundra, but at this point there wasn't much to do. The days passed pleasantly, but I felt uneasy. I'd heard nothing from Erskine since I left New York, no replies to the cables I sent almost daily. I was worried.

The *Distributor* left Alberta, entering the Northwest Territories, and docked at Fort Smith. Lord Tweedsmuir prepared to deliver his usual speech to a group of Eskimos. A radio operator came aboard and greeted me. "I'll bet you're the young lady I've been looking for," he said and handed me a telegram addressed to HONEYCHILE, ARCTIC CIRCLE, CANADA. "We thought this sounded like you," he added, grinning.

The message was brief: COME HOME AND MARRY ME. SIGNED SKINNY.

Almost any girl might have been thrilled to receive such a message from a lover, but I had not changed my mind on the subject of marriage. Erskine was moving out of his hotel room and into an apartment next to mine. In New York we went everywhere together. Everyone expected us to marry. Now here I was, thousands of miles away, feeling an intense rush of longing for my darling Skinny, but still not wanting to say yes.

The steamer left the Athabasca River and followed the

Mackenzie, dropping off goods and a dwindling number of passengers at each stop. After several days we arrived at Fort Norman. Two more cables were waiting for me—one from *Life*, the other from Erskine.

I opened *Life*'s cable first: REQUEST YOU CHARTER PLANE AND SHOOT ARCTIC OCEAN IN SUMMER. There was no question that I would accept the assignment.

The cable from Erskine begged me to take the next plane home and marry him. I understood that he would not be satisfied until I was completely his. My feelings were mixed, constantly changing. Erskine and his pleas felt far away, part of another life. I put the cable with the others. I had work to do, the Arctic Ocean to explore.

The *Distributor* left the Mackenzie and turned east, up Great Bear River. I kept my eye on the butterfly chrysalises that I'd nurtured from eggs to caterpillars. The cooler temperatures had slowed down the metamorphosis, but I knew that any day, at any hour, my beauties would be ready to emerge. If I missed that event, I'd have to start all over the following year.

Anticipating this, I found the captain, and with my most persuasive smile, I said, "Captain, I have an enormous favor to ask of you."

"What is it?" he asked gruffly.

"I'm in the midst of an important scientific project involving the life cycle of mourning cloak butterflies, and I wonder if you could possibly stop the engines when my butterflies begin to emerge, so that I can photograph them without the vibrations spoiling the focus." I offered another smile.

The captain gazed at me in astonishment. "Miss Bourke-White, I've been working these rivers for thirty years, I've never stopped a boat even if a man fell overboard, and now you want me to stop it for a damned butterfly?"

"Yes, please, captain."

He nodded briefly and walked away. I hoped that meant he'd agreed.

I taped the ten chrysalises to the rail of the deck, set up my equipment, and settled down to wait. The sun skimmed above the horizon and glowed dimly for a few minutes before soaring overhead again.

For the next few days I dozed in my deckchair, never actually sleeping. Passengers brought me food from the dining room. Lord Tweedsmuir passed by periodically, greeting me warmly and addressing me as Maggie, and loaned me books to help pass the time.

On a bright Sunday morning at the edge of the Arctic Circle, I detected the first wiggle and sent a message to the captain. The engines went still. The chrysalises began to split. His Excellency came to watch and to offer help. While I took picture after picture, ten butterflies had emerged, grandly unfolding their purple-black wings with broad yellow borders. The captain grumbled, the engines started up again, and I had a magnificent set of photographs.

◆◆

Before the steamer's final destination lay a thousand miles and a dozen more trading posts. The sight of a handful of decrepit wooden buildings and the sound of howling sled dogs greeted us at each stop. There was also at least one cable addressed to "Honeychile," delivered by a smirking radio operator who had probably shared the contents with everyone in the village.

We arrived at Port Brabant, a tiny hamlet spread out on a flat spit of land surrounded by the waters of Mackenzie Bay. His tour complete, Lord Tweedsmuir flew off to Ontario. I released the four surviving butterflies, and searched for a pilot willing to take me out over the Arctic Ocean. The only planes flying this far north belonged to the Royal Canadian Mail and accepted private passengers only when it didn't interfere with delivering the mail to these isolated outposts.

By good luck I met two other adventurous travelers: Archibald Lang Fleming, a bishop of the Church of England, and Dr. Thomas Wood, an English composer and travel writer. Known as Archibald the Arctic, the bishop was making his semiannual tour of the remotest churches in his diocese, and "Doc" was working on a book about Canada. The three of us negotiated with a handsome bush pilot, Art Rankin, to take us where we wanted to go in an ancient flying machine he'd named *Nyla*. Art rounded up a bewhiskered copilot named Billy, and the deal was done.

While the pilots made their preparations, I went sightseeing around Port Brabant. In the Hudson's Bay store I met a lonely trapper who told me sadly that I reminded him of his ex-wife. He had ordered a fur parka as a wedding gift for his bride, but she had taken one look at this godforsaken village and didn't stay long enough to claim it before she fled back to Minnesota. The Eskimo woman who had made the parka lived in the village of Coppermine, and if by chance I happened to visit Coppermine, the trapper said, the parka would be mine. He scrawled a note to present at the trading post, authorizing me to claim it.

An hour later the bishop, the composer, the pilot, the copilot, and I were on our way—first stop, Coppermine. On the ground again, Art and I made for the trading post that doubled as the post office. Art handed over the sack of mail, and I produced the trapper's letter.

Sewn from caribou fur, trimmed with white reindeer fur, and fringed with wolverine, the parka was one of the most elegant garments I'd ever owned. Archibald the Arctic used my camera to take my photograph.

We left Coppermine. Art had removed one of the doors of

Margaret loved clothes and considered this handmade fur parka the most elegant item in her wardrobe.

the plane and tied a rope around my waist so I wouldn't fall as I leaned out to take pictures. The scene below was perfect: dark water and floating ice bathed in a warm golden light. Then the picture suddenly vanished, and we were enveloped in featureless white.

Fog.

It was like being suspended inside a cloud. Every landmark disappeared, and it was impossible to tell up from down. The pilot had to descend quickly. He swooped low and climbed high, searching for a break in the blankness. No one spoke.

A small hole appeared in the white nothingness. Through it I glimpsed open sea, a narrow inlet, and a slender crescent of rock.

"That's it!" shouted Art above the roar of the motor. "We're going in!"

The old plane settled gently onto the water, and Art scrambled onto the rocky shore to tie it up. The rest of us followed gingerly, leaping from the pontoons to the shore without falling into the frigid waters.

"Now," announced Archibald the Arctic, "we shall have tea."

The bishop unpacked a tin pot from his valise and set off over the rocks to gather sticks, practically nonexistent in the Arctic, until he found enough to make a small fire. We had tea.

Art tried to radio for help. He knew where we were: one of the Lewes Islands, some three hundred miles from any sort of human habitation. Every hour on the hour, the radio operator back in Coppermine tried to reach us: "Art Rankin on *Nyla*, please respond. Visibility remains zero. Art Rankin, please respond."

We could hear *him*, but he could not hear *us*. *Nyla*'s signal was not strong enough to reach Coppermine.

"How long do these fogs hang around?" I asked.

"Sometimes for weeks," Art said matter-of-factly, and I was sorry I'd asked.

We took stock of our resources: enough rations to sustain life for one man for twenty days. There were five of us.

Then Billy, the copilot, found a fresh-water spring. "A blessing," said the bishop.

It had felt strange to pack a ski suit when I was leaving New York in July. Now I was glad I had it, and my new fur parka, too. Archibald the Arctic proved to be an entertaining storyteller. Doc made up songs and taught them to us, and we sang. We built cairns and pelted them with pebbles. Art was a deadeye shot. I took pictures in the odd, disorienting light. Then we slept a little and tried not to think about the fog.

The radio operator in Coppermine reported continuing zero visibility, and on one broadcast added that he had a cable for somebody named Honeychile: WHEN ARE YOU COMING HOME? SIGNED SKINNY.

"Tell him to come up here," muttered Billy, who by then knew my story. "We've got a bishop to marry you and two witnesses besides."

Suddenly the fog thinned and lifted slightly. Art hustled us into the plane. We were scarcely airborne when the fog vanished and gave way to lashing rain. For two hours *Nyla* fought her way through the storm. It was like being underwater. We were all quiet, for we knew the gas gauge must be falling, and night was falling, and if a miracle didn't occur soon, we too would be falling, falling . . .

But a miracle *did* occur. Art sighted a few dots on the tundra that might be a settlement. He circled, dropped, and landed on a river. We piled out onto another rocky shore, grateful beyond words—except Archibald the Arctic, who had a number of words appropriate for the occasion, to which we all added "Amen!"

The settlement was deserted, except for a sole Eskimo who explained in his language that everyone had gone to fish camp and would be back in a few weeks with enough fish to feed the village through the winter. Billy translated for us: We were guests of the village, and we were to help ourselves to whatever we needed.

Ravenous, we dined on a cache of canned meat and beans. We discovered a dusty old Victrola and a few records, only slightly warped, and we cranked it up and danced. I had four willing partners. Far more important, though, was a supply of gasoline left behind by whalers. It was enough to get the intrepid *Nyla* into the air again.

We flew to Aklavik, not far from Port Brabant, where we'd begun our adventure. I caught a flight to Yellowknife, cabled Erskine that I was on my way home, and got a good night's sleep, my first in a real bed in a month.

The next morning in the Chicago airport I was looking for my flight to New York. A cacophony of urgent messages and muffled announcements blared over the loudspeaker, and I ignored them until one in particular, repeated for the third time, finally registered: "Paging Child Bride, please stop at the ticket counter for a message."

Child Bride? I could guess who that might be. I identified myself—"I'm Child Bride," I said, feeling slightly ridiculous—and opened the telegram:

WELCOME, WELCOME, WELCOME, WELCOME.

26

Promises—1938

ERSKINE WAS GLAD TO HAVE ME BACK HOME, I was glad to be there, and for a while everything went smoothly, as long as I didn't travel on assignment. Then, early in the new year, Erskine received notice that his wife, Helen, had finally filed for divorce, and he began again to pressure me to marry him. The more tightly he tried to hold on to me, the more I struggled to hold on to my freedom. And when I did struggle, he fell into a dark depression or exploded with rage. I tried to leave him, but he would not give up. He couldn't bear to be without me! He wouldn't let me go!

And so I stayed. *For now,* I told myself. *I'll stay for now.*

The editors at *Life* had been so pleased by the pictures I'd brought from my month in the Arctic that they ran two stories in the same issue—eight pages about Lord Tweedsmuir and his tour through the Northwest Territories, and another three pages on Archibald the Arctic. It was the first time *Life* had printed two stories by the same photographer in one issue.

I was ready for my next big assignment, and I got it.

Newspaper headlines in the winter of 1938 showed that Europe was on the brink of war. German troops had entered Austria, and Hitler was threatening to invade Czechoslovakia and wipe it off the map. In Spain, Francisco Franco's fascists were taking control of Spain.

Life's editors wanted me to travel to Europe to cover these stories, and I was eager to go.

The timing was right. Erskine and I had already begun to talk about doing another book together. He had a title for it: *North of the Danube*. I organized my trip around the project and made all the plans. We sailed for Europe at the end of March.

We made our way through cities and villages and farmland, meeting with people and listening to their stories as we had in the American South, taking photographs and sending them back to *Life*. I was recording history as it was happening.

But at every step I had to keep one eye on Erskine. Without warning and for no reason I could see, he would sink into a black mood that seemed to drag everyone else down. His erratic behavior put off even the generous people who helped us, and that hindered my own work. I had counted on the easy way I'd had with my subjects as we'd traveled through the South for our first book. Now Erskine's unpredictable mood changes distracted me. I could not give my complete attention to the people I was photographing, and it showed in their faces.

After nearly five months in Europe we sailed for home. When the *Aquitania* docked in New York harbor at the end of August, reporters and photographers swarmed the decks. We were a celebrity couple, Erskine for his writing and I for my photographs, and we were peppered with questions—not sensible questions about what we had witnessed in Europe, but pointless ones. "Miss Bourke-White! When are you going to marry Mr. Caldwell?"

"I'm not going to get married, no matter how much it might

please the press corps," I snapped. "I like being single."

My sarcastic response to the reporters didn't faze Erskine. His divorce from Helen had become final while we were away. He continued his campaign with gifts and flowers and singing telegrams, still begging me to marry him, still trying to wear me down.

And I kept saying no.

We decided to get out of the city for the summer and rented a cottage in Connecticut. Erskine's writing went so well there that we bought a house together and called it "Horseplay Hill." Our new neighbors assumed we were married, and we never told them differently.

But still I said no.

All those years when I was striving to make a name for myself, I had sworn that I would not marry. I had achieved my goal. Thanks to *Life* magazine, my photographs and I were famous. For six more months I wrestled with the question: *Why not marry?* I was thirty-four, I truly loved Erskine; maybe I needed him as much as he needed me. It had become almost too much trouble *not* to be married.

On Sunday night, February 26, 1939, I stopped agonizing. I said yes.

Having come to that momentous decision, neither of us was willing to wait even one more day. Very early the next morning we were at the airport, ready to fly on the first plane to Nevada, where we could get a marriage license without the usual three-day delay. Erskine brought champagne to drink on the flight, but I had something more important in mind.

"I want to draw up a contract listing certain conditions of our marriage," I told Erskine as we flew west. "We can drink champagne later."

My bridegroom seemed surprised, but I insisted. "We need

211

to be absolutely clear about certain things."

"Such as?"

I ticked them off on my fingers. One, that if a disagreement came up, we would discuss it and solve the problem before bedtime. Two, that he would treat my friends as well as he did his own. Three, that he would try to control his moods. Four, and this was the most important: that he would not try to interfere with my work.

I wrote it, and without even looking at it, Erskine signed it.

The pilot announced that we were stopping for fuel in Reno. "Shall we get married here?" Erskine asked, and I said, "Skinny, nobody gets married in Reno! This is where people get divorced!"

We borrowed a map from the pilot and looked for a town within a hundred miles that sounded more appealing. Silver City had a nice name. When the plane landed in Reno, we hurried to the courthouse to get our license and hailed a taxi to drive us to Silver City. The driver pointed out that Silver City was a ghost town. We'd have to take a minister with us, and another witness as well.

"Where will we find a minister?" Erskine asked the cabbie.

"Carson City," said the helpful cabbie. "It's the state capital. We'll find somebody there."

And we did. Or rather, the cab driver did—a member of the state legislature, who happened to be sitting in the lobby of a hotel near the capitol. The lawmaker, authorized to perform a marriage ceremony, was delighted to be of assistance and climbed into the taxi with us. It was late afternoon when we pulled into Silver City, with not a soul in sight. The fact that it seemed completely deserted made it as charming as a stage set, and we knew immediately it was the right place. There was no time to lose in finding a church, because Erskine was determined that the knot would be tied before sundown.

We did find a lovely old church, but when Erskine tried the weathered wooden door, it was locked. The cab driver was undaunted. He would find a key! The legislator pointed out a tobacco shop with a faded OPEN sign in the window. I hurried inside. "Do you happen to know how we can get into the church?" I asked the owner, whose face was as weathered as the church door. "It's terribly important!"

The tobacconist miraculously produced a key to the church from her apron pocket, and she volunteered to serve as our second witness. Five of us packed into the taxi, and back to the church we roared. The tobacconist turned the iron key in the rusty lock, and the door creaked open. A delicate blanket of dust lay over the wooden pews. Late afternoon sun filtered through unwashed windows and sparrows flitted among the rafters. We stood in front of the bare altar, Erskine pulled a wedding ring out of his pocket, the legislator recited whatever parts of the ceremony he knew by heart, and our witnesses nodded and smiled as though they were our closest relatives.

After the ceremony the others went outside to wait. Erskine and I stood alone, holding hands, gazing out over the stark landscape of mesas and bluffs and desert, like unfinished sculptures in the fading light. I squeezed my new husband's hand, and whispered, "I love you, Skinny." My throat tightened with a rush of tenderness for the gentle man by my side who had waited so long for this moment.

Our grinning cabbie dropped the tobacconist off at her shop and drove the state representative to his hotel in Carson City, where we decided to spend the night. The next morning we hired a private plane to fly us on to San Francisco, and that afternoon we sailed on the SS *Lurline* for a honeymoon in Hawaii.

Once again I was somebody's wife, and if I had any misgivings, I ignored them.

27

Europe at War—1939

OUR FIRST MONTHS AS HUSBAND AND WIFE WERE all I could have reasonably wished for. Our book, *North of the Danube*, was praised when it came out, but I knew it wasn't nearly as good as *You Have Seen Their Faces*. For my sake Erskine struggled to tame his unpredictable moods. I didn't take on assignments that involved being away from home for long stretches, but there was too much happening in the world. I simply could not sit at home with the situation in Europe worsening by the day. I had to be in the midst of the action. My reputation depended on it, no matter what Erskine said.

Late in the fall of 1939, I left for London. The good-byes were harder than ever. Erskine's cables addressed to "Child Bride" found me there, and when I moved on to Rumania in December, even those he dispatched to "Honeychile" somehow found their destination. I missed our first wedding anniversary at the end of February, and in March 1940, I reached Syria by way of Turkey; from there I intended to go on to Italy. I sent a constant stream of cables, assuring my husband of my love, my adoration. It didn't help. He begged me to come home. He said that he could not deal with the loneliness, and I wasn't sure I could deal with his needing me so much.

Meanwhile, things were not working out with *Life* the way they had in the past and the way I wanted. Where were the credit lines for my photographs? *Life*'s new policy of publishing photographs anonymously angered me. More photographers were being hired. Why were some of my pictures being set aside to make room for theirs? Where was the fame I deserved? My relationship with Harry Luce had cooled, and I began to have doubts about whether I wanted to stay with *Life*.

A daily newspaper called *PM* would be launched soon, and I was offered a job. It promised to be more inventive, more daring, more progressive than any other newspaper out there—and it sounded exciting and more interesting than *Life*. It would be a new challenge, a new adventure, and I wanted to be part of the "new." The pay was not as good, but it would mean less travel and a wider audience, and Erskine and I could work together on stories.

I made the decision to resign from *Life* and cabled Harry Luce from Syria. He was not pleased that I was planning to leave his magazine for an archrival. In fact, he was furious. But he did nothing to change the situation and cabled back: GOOD LUCK. HENRY LUCE.

After only a few months, *PM* flopped. Nothing had worked out. I went back to *Life*. Harry didn't turn me away, but neither did he give me a warm welcome. But there was no time to lick my wounds. In 1941, Germany was preparing to invade Russia, and *Life*'s picture editor, Wilson Hicks, wanted me to be there when the invasion began. I knew how things worked in Russia, and I'd have no trouble getting permission to photograph. Erskine and I could travel together. Erskine was one of America's most important writers, and his stories and novels were well known in Russia.

Because the German army had overrun Europe in 1940, we couldn't simply take an ocean liner across the Atlantic to Cherbourg or Southampton and board a train to Moscow.

Instead, we would fly west from California to China and work our way into Russia, ultimately to Moscow.

I spent a month figuring out what equipment I'd need. Erskine and I took off from Los Angeles in March 1941 on a flight to Hong Kong with 617 pounds of luggage. All but seventeen pounds were mine. Erskine knew how to travel light. From Hong Kong we flew to Chungking, and then across the Gobi Desert. From a sand-swept little town on the border, we made the last leg of the journey into Russia. It took us a full thirty-one days, most of that time spent trying to cut through red tape, find planes that were capable of flying, wait out sandstorms, or simply *wait*.

On June 22, a month after our arrival, while we were traveling in the Ukraine, we heard the news: German troops had invaded. We jumped onto a train headed for Moscow.

The Russian military had forbidden the use of cameras, and anyone seen with one could be arrested and sent to prison. The order cancelled out my official permission to take pictures. I had to find a way around it, and I had to get to the center of the action and figure out a way to stay there.

We spent our first nights in a hotel with a balcony overlooking Red Square and the Kremlin, turreted government buildings, and churches with colorful onion-shaped domes. If we had been tourists, this would have been a prime view of Moscow. Now I had a prime view of bombs falling on the city. The American ambassador came to try to persuade us to leave; there were two seats on the train to Vladivostok.

"For your own safety, Mrs. Caldwell," he said.

We turned them down. I told him, "We were sent here to do a job, and we're going to do it." I added, "And the name is Margaret Bourke-White."

The military issued another order: when the sirens began screaming, everyone had to take shelter in the subways. Wardens searched our hotel, room by room, to make sure everyone was out. The first time, Erskine and I obeyed the order, spending the night in a huge underground subway station with thousands of Muscovites.

"Listen, Skinny," I told him when we were allowed to leave the next morning, "this is no way to cover a war we traveled thousands of miles to witness. I'm not doing this again."

Dodging military patrols, I sneaked over to the American embassy, where the Russians had no authority to order us anywhere, and climbed out on the roof. German bombers droned overhead. The view was spectacular, but it offered no protection. I hunkered down near an airshaft and watched the Luftwaffe planes roar over with their payloads. A kind of sixth sense told me that a bomb was about to fall nearby. I dived through an open window and flung myself on the floor as far from the window as I could, protecting my camera with my body. The blast came, shattering the windows. Glass fragments fell on me like rain. When the roar of engines had faded, I crept down the sweeping staircase, broken glass crunching under my feet, and took pictures of the wreckage and wired them to *Life*. These were the first photographs of the bombing of Moscow to be published in the United States.

Our hotel suite was furnished with a grand piano, a marble bust of Napoleon, and a magnificent white bearskin rug. The sitting room became my workshop. I filled the bathtub with developing trays and hung wet negatives on cords strung among the overhead pipes, hoping a siren wouldn't go off and interrupt a process that must not, under any circumstances, be interrupted. When a siren did sound and an air-raid warden burst in to make sure we weren't breaking the rules, I rolled under the bed and Erskine draped the bearskin over his head and shoulders and ducked behind the sofa. Did the warden not notice the glassy-eyed polar bear, or did he choose not to? Eventually he left us alone.

Crouching low to avoid being spotted by soldiers stationed in Red Square below, I set up cameras on the balcony, two facing in opposite directions to take in the sky and two more on the windowsill. A fifth camera was stored in the basement of the embassy, in case the others were destroyed. As the Germans bombed Moscow for twenty-two nights, I took photographs, developed and printed them, got them past the censors, and sent them to my editor in the United States.

◆◆

My biggest challenge was to photograph Josef Stalin. Every time I'd asked permission, I was turned down. Then President Roosevelt's personal envoy arrived in Moscow. I had met him once before, and he remembered me. I dogged his steps, begging him to intervene, until he agreed to do what he could.

"All right, Margaret," the envoy reported at last. "You've got permission."

I'd heard that Russians like red, and I dug out from my luggage a red bow to wear in my hair. On the day of my appointment with Stalin I paced outside his office for two hours before I was finally admitted. The much-feared dictator turned out to be short, pockmarked, and unimposing—the opposite of what I expected. But nothing I did could make that stone face register any expression. Then, when I crouched to make some low shots, a handful of little flashbulbs spilled out of my pocket, and I went down on my hands and knees to gather them up. This appeared to amuse Stalin. A hint of a smile appeared beneath his brushy mustache and lasted just long enough for me to snap the shutter twice before it vanished. I had what I wanted.

The German *Luftwaffe* was about to launch another air raid, the sirens were already going off, and I couldn't risk having the wardens burst into my hotel bathroom while I was developing these precious pictures. I had my driver take me to the embassy instead. It was deserted; everyone had gone off to shelters. The driver helped me set up a makeshift darkroom in the servants' bathroom. I scribbled some notes to the photo editor, packed up the prints, and left the package for President Roosevelt's envoy to deliver to the *Life* offices when he flew home the next day.

◆ ◆

My major goal was to get to the front where the fighting was intense and both Russians and Germans were taking heavy losses. But no matter how many strings I tried to pull, I was always turned down. Time was running out. Erskine and I would soon have to leave for commitments back in the United States

Suddenly permission was granted. A five-car convoy took us and a group of British and American correspondents to the Smolensk front, some two hundred miles west of Moscow. I had less than a week to accomplish my goal. Six days of pelting rain and mud up to my knees made picture-taking nearly impossible. On the last day the weather cleared. Wearing my red coat turned inside out so that I wouldn't be a target for German riflemen, I got photographs of a bombed-out town, of its dead and dying victims and grieving survivors of another air raid. When I developed those negatives, I couldn't bear to look at them.

Erskine and I began our journey home. At a port on the Arctic Ocean we boarded a cargo ship traveling in a convoy to Scotland; from there we flew to Portugal. Lisbon was crowded with Americans who had waited weeks to book a flight to the United States. We went to the airline office to inquire about our reservations. There was, indeed, a seat for Mr. Caldwell, but nothing for Mrs. Caldwell. The only other unclaimed seat was for a lady from Russia. I asked the lady's name.

The clerk looked it up. "Margaret Bourke-White," he said.

◆ ◆

Erskine had wired ahead to our secretary to have Sunday

dinner ready for us when we arrived in New York, chicken and steak and "all manner of fresh fruits and vegetables." But before dessert, I left for the airport again without a chance to recover from the nearly eight-month journey. I was starting off on a lecture tour that would take me across the country, speaking to women's groups. I would be paid well, but it was not just the money: I planned to use the lectures as a first draft of a book I wanted to write without Erskine's collaboration. I would call it *Russia at War*.

There was another compelling reason for the lecture tour: I needed to get away from Erskine. While I raced from one speaking engagement to the next, Erskine's volatile moods veered from bright sun to ominous clouds in a matter of seconds. At each stop another message waited for me, as he alternately ordered and coaxed me to move with him to a house we'd bought in the Arizona desert.

"I want to settle down," he argued. "I've always said a writer's life is good for only about ten years, and then it's time to switch gears."

I didn't believe that was true. And it certainly was not true of photographers.

When Japan bombed Pearl Harbor on December 7, 1941, settling down was the last thing I wanted to do. Our country was at war, and within days the president declared war on Germany, too.

"Skinny, they're going to need photographers to take pictures and send them back so the people at home know what's going on," I explained. "I've got to do this, if they'll let me."

"It's always what *you* want, isn't it, Kit?" Erskine said bitterly. "You always call the shots."

I'd given up arguing with him. I sensed that he had always been jealous of my work, even though he was proud of it, but he left no doubt that he was jealous of *Life* for the claim it had on my time and energy. I'd learned to let it go. But I didn't know how much longer I could do that.

◆ ◆

Early in the spring of 1942 I flew to New York, walked into *Life*'s offices, and went straight to the picture editor's desk. Wilson Hicks looked up and flashed a pleased grin. "Maggie, hello! Sit down! Bring me up to date!"

I leaned my hands on Hicks's desk and brought my eyes level with his. "I won't sit until you promise to send me to Europe," I said. "I want an overseas assignment to cover this war. You know I have skills that could be important to the war effort."

Hicks's eyebrows shot up. "OK," he said. "But in the meantime, please sit down while we figure out how to do this."

It took longer than I would have liked—I always wanted things to happen more or less instantaneously—but there were a lot of *i*'s to be dotted and *t*'s to be crossed until Hicks and Harry Luce succeeded in having me accredited as a war correspondent by the Pentagon. I pleaded and nagged, begged and bullied every day until I got the accreditation. I would shoot pictures for the Army Air Forces, and *Life* had permission to use the pictures after they'd been cleared by the censors.

Obviously, I needed a uniform. Although I was the first woman war correspondent, I would not be the only one, and I pointed out that we needed to be properly attired if we were to be recognized as professionals. The War College went to work on the design, with my suggestions. I would have a blouse—the military word for jacket—and slacks, and also a skirt of the same olive drab material for everyday wear. I also had "dress pinks," actually a rosy gray, for formal occasions. A shoulder patch identified me as a war correspondent, insignia marked my rank as first lieutenant, and a jaunty flight cap matched my uniform.

I could not have felt any prouder when I wore that uniform for the first time. Jubilant, too, because I had what I wanted.

When I was sure there would be no more bureaucratic foul-ups, I flew back to our home in Arizona to wait for my orders and to spend time with Erskine. In early August my orders came through. I was to leave for England. Our last few days together were warm and affectionate but cooled as the hour of my departure approached. Erskine was sunk in one of his black, bleak moods when I left. Neither of us had any idea how long I'd be gone.

United States at War—1942

I WAS BILLETED AT A SECRET BOMBER BASE OUTSIDE OF London, staying in the officers' quarters in a cell-like room with a cot, a coke-burning stove, and a washstand. I arrived around the same time as the B-17 bombers. I was out on the runway to photograph the Flying Fortresses, as they were called, when they took off on their first mission—thirteen of them—and I was there and counting them as all thirteen returned.

I quickly became part of the team, and the crew of one of the B-17s asked me to name their plane. The name I proposed was *Flying Flit Gun*. "Flit" was a widely-used bug spray, and a Flit Gun was the hand-pumped sprayer. The "bugs" to be "sprayed" with bombs were caricatures of our enemies—Germany's Hitler, Italy's Mussolini, and Japan's Hirohito—painted on the plane's fuselage. A proper christening was arranged, which usually meant smashing a bottle of champagne on the bow of a newly launched ship, but this was a plane, not a ship, and we had no champagne. I climbed a tall ladder in my "dress pinks" skirt, loudly proclaimed, "I christen thee *Flying Flit Gun*," and smashed a bottle of Coca-Cola on one of the bomber's guns. A band played, and the commanding officer, Colonel Atkinson, made a speech. I always felt pride and relief when *Flying Flit Gun* made it back safely from another bombing run.

Sometimes I was sent on special assignments to London—photographing Prime Minister Winston Churchill on his birthday, for one—but making portraits was not the reason I was there. I wanted to witness the war up close. I wanted to fly on a combat mission, but my requests were denied. I could go on practice runs, but not on a real bombing mission. I knew why. "The High Command does not wish to expose women to the dangers of war." I kept trying.

At the same time, I had something much more deeply distressing to deal with: my husband. When I left for England, our marriage was fraying—I could see that—but I wanted to believe that it was still intact. Erskine wrote to me often, but our letters crossed in the transatlantic mail, and the latest letter from Erskine was never a response to my most recent letter to him.

He was lonely, he said. He had trouble writing when I was away, and he pleaded with me to finish up whatever I was doing and hurry home. He loved me, he wrote. He would always love me. He said I was his truest, deepest love.

Suddenly his tone changed. At the beginning of October I received a terse cable stating that the last he'd heard from me was a letter on the tenth of September and a wire on the twentieth. Five weeks of silence followed. On November 9 I received another cable.

He had reached a difficult decision, the most difficult of his life, he wired—PARTNERSHIP MUST DISSOLVE IMMEDIATELY. The situation was unbearable, he could see no future for it, and nothing could be done to change it. He was truly sorry, Erskine stated, and was himself inconsolable.

That was all.

I was completely thrown off balance, but I did not want anyone to know how badly shaken I was. I wired back and asked him to explain his reasons more fully. Was there someone else? Two days later I had Erskine's reply. It didn't offer much of an explanation, except to say that both present and future were dismal. It ended, SUCH IS LONELINESS.

I shot back that this answer was really no answer at all. Then I waited. Perhaps I should have been devastated, but in fact I felt relieved. I would no longer have to worry about what sort of mood he was in, how he would behave around other people, or how he would relate to me. After a week had passed, I wrote to my lawyer as my husband had suggested, telling the lawyer that the only thing I wanted from the marriage was the house in Connecticut. We hadn't spent much time there recently, but I liked it, and I'd need a home when the war ended. Erskine agreed.

And that was that. My marriage was over. Work would be my salvation, as it always had been.

I was about to launch another campaign to get myself on board a bombing mission when I heard a rumor that the Allies were planning to invade North Africa. The plan was top secret—no one knew, certainly not my *Life* editors. I simply *had* to be involved. Luck was on my side: General Atkinson would command the invasion—he was promoted from colonel soon after he'd given the speech at the christening of *Flying Flit Gun*. I knew him well, and it wasn't hard to get his permission.

I assumed I'd fly in one of the B-17s, preferably the *Flit Gun*, but the top brass vetoed that idea. "It's too dangerous, Margaret," General Atkinson said flatly when I tried to change his mind. "You'll travel in a convoy. It's much safer."

It was a very large convoy with an aircraft carrier, troopships, destroyers, and smaller escort ships called corvettes. I was assigned to a troopship that had formerly been a luxury liner, with chandeliers and plush-covered divans and a sweeping marble staircase. Somehow they had managed to shoehorn six thousand British and American troops onto this *grande dame* of a vessel, plus four hundred Scottish nurses, five WAACs—the Women's Army Auxiliary Corps—and Captain Kay Summersby, a beautiful Irish girl who served as chauffeur for General Dwight Eisenhower, who was in charge of the invasion.

Off we sailed, straight into the teeth of one of the most violent storms the ship's captain could remember. Day after day we zigged and zagged toward Gibraltar and the Mediterranean, tossed around like bathtub toys, rising and plunging through towering waves. The grand piano rumbled across the floor, tables and chairs became airborne missiles. Almost everyone was horribly seasick, but for some reason I was immune.

No matter how bad it got, the ship's captain insisted that we endure regular lifeboat drills. They were torture for all those poor seasick souls who had to drag themselves out of their bunks, march to their assigned lifeboat stations, and wait, silent and attentive for a quarter of an hour as they were dashed with freezing spray, until they were allowed to totter back to their cabins.

As soon as we were through the Strait of Gibraltar and entered the Mediterranean, the sea became calm. Those of us with sturdier stomachs who had braved the grand saloon twice a day for a meal prepared by the unflappable galley crew told stories of flying crockery that made every meal dangerous. But all that changed. We relaxed. We laughed. We were due to land in North Africa the next day. I made sure my cameras and lenses were in order and rearranged the contents of my musette bag, a rubberized canvas shoulder bag that we'd each been issued and instructed to keep stocked with extra socks, chocolate, soap, first aid supplies, and a few emergency rations. I decided that an extra camera and film qualified as an emergency supply.

A farewell party was in raucous progress in the grand saloon. Rumors circulated that a German U-boat had been sighted earlier in the day. It was likely there were others, as they often traveled in "wolfpacks" and had been shadowing our convoy for three days, since we'd escaped the storm and entered the Mediterranean. The destroyer had taken out one submarine. "That leaves the rest of the wolves to worry about," commented a junior officer as the party wound down.

"Good night!" we called out cheerfully as we headed below to our bunks. "Good night!"

Most of us were asleep an hour later when the German torpedo found its mark.

. . . It has been a long, long night of hunger, cold, and fatigue. Shivering in my soaking wet officer's coat, I fear for my own life, but I also grapple with the sickening knowledge that men and women have been dying all around me since we abandoned ship, and I can do nothing to save them.

I wonder if I will die. I wonder if Erskine will grieve for me if I do.

Hours drag by. After sunrise I take pictures. It's the only thing I know to do.

In midafternoon someone spots a flying boat, a large seaplane. It flies low over us, waggling its wings, and we wave back, assuring each other that help will come soon. The afternoon fades and the sun sinks lower, lower. There is no sign of rescuers. It won't be long before darkness descends, and they won't be able to find us. No one wants to speak about this.

Late in the day a destroyer appears, a mere speck on the horizon. It's possible that they don't know exactly where we are. It's possible there's another German U-boat out there, another deadly torpedo. We will the ship to come faster. We will it to see us. And then it is there, and we're cheering, dizzy with relief. By nightfall we've been hauled aboard the crowded ship, grateful to be warm and dry with food in our stomachs and a place to sleep.

Exhausted but not yet ready to sleep, I walk out on deck and stand beneath the glittering bowl of the heavens as the destroyer slices through the silent waters of the Mediterranean toward the coast of North Africa. I have survived. For now I am safe, but the world is at war, and I have much more work to do.

Margaret emerged from her linsey-woolsey
girlhood as a glamourous woman and a
famous photographer.

Note from the Author

Girl with a Camera is a work of fiction based on the real life of Margaret Bourke-White. I've ended my story in December 1942, near the midpoint of her career with many years of exhilarating adventures and triumphant achievements still ahead.

After her rescue, Margaret and the others on board the destroyer landed in Algiers, where she had the good fortune to run into General Atkinson, the same officer who had cleared her to travel with the troops to North Africa. The general gave her permission to go on a bombing mission. Issued a fleece-lined leather flight suit, she took pictures from the window of a Flying Fortress as the bombs were dropped.

I remember as a child seeing a photograph in *Life* of Margaret in her flight suit—it seemed that everyone followed the progress of the war in the pages of that magazine. My father had enlisted in the Army Air Forces soon after the Japanese bombed Pearl Harbor, and he'd received his overseas orders in the fall of 1942. My mother and I saw him off at the railroad station in my home-town. He flew first to England, then to North Africa, and he must have arrived there about the same time that Margaret did.

Margaret Bourke-White caused a sensation wherever she went, and as I was working on this book I began to wonder if Lieutenant Meyer had ever met the glamorous photographer. Then I found one of his missing wartime diaries. In an entry my father made late in December 1942 I found a reference to

Scottish nurses whose ship had been torpedoed. A few pages on he mentioned having coffee with General Atkinson. No mention, though, of Margaret Bourke-White.

In the spring of 1943 she returned to the States, but after only two months she was agitating to get back to the war. Early in September Margaret returned to North Africa and received her orders to join Allied troops who had moved on to Italy, where they were fighting to drive out the Germans. For months she flew reconnaissance missions and slept in foxholes, repeatedly risking her life to get the pictures she wanted.

As she prepared to leave Italy in 1943, she photographed a field hospital under bombardment. The photographs were sent to the Pentagon in Washington to be cleared by the censors, but somehow they were lost and never found. Margaret believed this was one of her most important stories, and it was a painful loss she never forgot. A few months later, when most of the other reporters and photographers had moved on to cover the fighting in France, Margaret was allowed to return to Italy, where the fighting stubbornly continued. She was in Rome until early 1945, when she left for Germany and photographed the liberation of the concentration camp at Buchenwald. Her pictures of the atrocities committed there were among the first seen in America. As the war came to a close, Margaret was assigned to photograph German factories as they were being captured. Then she flew home, staying long enough to write another book, *Dear Fatherland, Rest Quietly*, expressing her anger at Germany. Although Margaret never referred publicly to herself as being "half Jewish," the prejudice against Jews that had been instilled in her by her mother had been eradicated even before she witnessed the atrocities committed by the Nazis against the Jews.

Margaret's next *Life* assignment took her to India in 1946 and again in 1947, to photograph Mahatma Gandhi as the subcontinent was gaining its independence from the British Empire. In 1949, she traveled with her camera to South Africa to document conditions in the gold and diamond mines. After that experience, she vowed she'd never wear gold or diamonds again.

During the early 1950s, when writers and actors and photographers and ordinary citizens were being investigated by a Congressional committee for their supposedly pro-Communist activities and beliefs, Margaret found herself on the list. Determined to clear her name, she persuaded *Life* to send her to Korea to do a story that would demonstrate beyond doubt her loyalty to the principles of democracy.

About this time Margaret began to notice a weakness in her leg and clumsiness in her hands. The symptoms worsened, and she was eventually diagnosed with Parkinson's, a progressive disease that affects the brain's ability to control the body's movements. Even as her condition deteriorated, Margaret kept working, until in 1957 she was no longer able to accept assignments from *Life*.

Not long after Margaret's ship had been torpedoed off the coast of North Africa and she was rescued, she received a letter from her lawyer. Enclosed was a newspaper article that reported the marriage of Erskine Caldwell to a college student in Arizona. It was her former husband's third marriage; a few years later he married for the fourth time.

Margaret did not marry again, but she did fall in love several times—with an American major in Italy who did not survive the war, with a brilliant Russian violinist, with an army colonel stationed in Japan—and there were other, less serious, relationships. Mostly, though, she lived alone in her Connecticut home, surrounded by mementoes of her many trips, where she wrote, entertained friends when she wasn't immersed in writing her next book, and struggled valiantly against the inexorable progress of her disease. Margaret Bourke-White died August 27, 1971, at the age of sixty-seven.

I have drawn the outline of her life and filled in the details from various sources: her autobiography, *Portrait of Myself*; *Margaret Bourke-White: A Biography*, by Vicki Goldberg; her high school yearbook, and some of her personal papers from the Special Collections Library at Syracuse University. That collection is voluminous. I was happiest when I discovered gems like the poem she wrote when she was eleven, "Flit on, lovely butterfly," carefully saved by her mother. Another gratifying moment occurred when I dug up a copy of her high-school yearbook with the words of the class song she helped write and the name of the co-author, Jack Daniels.

I didn't alter facts, but because this is a novel, I did invent certain details (such as Margaret's prize-winning story) and a few minor characters, and I assigned names to characters who were not named specifically in my sources. For example, Tubby Luf was real; Sara Jane Cassidy was my creation.

Carolyn Meyer
Albuquerque, New Mexico

Carolyn Meyer is the best-selling, award-winning author of numerous novels for children and young adults, many of them on courageous women of the past. *Diary of a Waitress*, about the Harvey Girls of the American West, was also published by Calkins Creek. She lives in Albuquerque, New Mexico. Visit her at readcarolyn.com

Picture Credits

Getty Images/Photo by Margaret Bourke-White: 193; 198–199; 205

Getty Images/Photo by Alfred Eisenstaedt: 230

Library of Congress, Prints and Photographs Division: LC-DIG-ppmsca-19361: 4; LC-DIG-ppmsca-15839: 76